W9-DEV-684

FIREWORKS

Should We See It from the Side or the Bottom?

Hitoshi One

original screenplay: Shunji Iwai

YEN ON

New York

FIREWORKS

Should We See It from the Side or the Bottom?

FIREWORKS

Should We See It from the Side or the Bottom?

Shunji Iwai, Hitoshi One

Translation by Stephen Kohler

This book is a work of fiction. Names, characters, places, and incidents are the product of the author's imagination or are used fictitiously. Any resemblance to actual events, locales, or persons, living or dead, is coincidental.

Fireworks, Should We See It from the Side or the Bottom?
© Shunji Iwai, Hitoshi One 2017
© 2017 TOHO CO., LTD. / Aniplex Inc. / KADOKAWA CORPORATION / TOY'S FACTORY INC. / East Japan Marketing & Communications, Inc. / Lawson HMV Entertainment, Inc. / LINE Corporation
First published in Japan in 2017 by KADOKAWA CORPORATION, Tokyo.
English translation rights arranged with KADOKAWA CORPORATION, Tokyo through TUTTLE-MORI AGENCY, INC., Tokyo.

English translation © 2018 by Yen Press, LLC

Yen Press, LLC supports the right to free expression and the value of copyright. The purpose of copyright is to encourage writers and artists to produce the creative works that enrich our culture.

The scanning, uploading, and distribution of this book without permission is a theft of the author's intellectual property. If you would like permission to use material from the book (other than for review purposes), please contact the publisher. Thank you for your support of the author's rights.

Yen On
1290 Avenue of the Americas
New York, NY 10104

Visit us at yenpress.com
facebook.com/yenpress
twitter.com/yenpress
yenpress.tumblr.com
instagram.com/yenpress

First Yen On Edition: August 2018

Yen On is an imprint of Yen Press, LLC.
The Yen On name and logo are trademarks of Yen Press, LLC.

The publisher is not responsible for websites (or their content) that are not owned by the publisher.

Library of Congress Cataloging-in-Publication Data
Names: Iwai, Shunji, 1963– author. | One, Hitoshi, author. | Kohler, Stephen, translator.
Title: Fireworks, should we see it from the side or the bottom? / original screenplay by Shunji Iwai ; Hitoshi One ; translation by Stephen Kohler.
Description: First Yen On edition. | New York : Yen On, August 2018.
Identifiers: LCCN 2018017688 | ISBN 9781975353261 (hardcover)
Subjects: CYAC: Friendship—Fiction. | Love—Fiction. | Summer—Fiction.
Classification: LCC PZ7.1.O637 Fi 2018 | DDC [Fic]—dc23
LC record available at https://lccn.loc.gov/2018017688

ISBNs: 978-1-9753-5326-1 (hardcover)
978-1-9753-8221-6 (ebook)

1 3 5 7 9 10 8 6 4 2

LSC-C
Printed in the United States of America

Contents

When I was little, I could keep my eyes open underwater.

I could see everything around me clearly, even without goggles or a swim mask. Right before my eyes, bubbles large and small rushed this way and that, then burst softly. It was as if I were watching a silent fireworks display.

I believed that if I could hold my breath long enough, I'd be able to pass through the water into another world.

But the tightness in my chest would always force me up. My face would break through the water's surface, and I'd be met with bright-blue sky and white clouds. My world of silence would be gone, and I'd be thrust once again into deafening reality, with its school bells and screaming cicadas.

There's only one world, after all.

Obviously.

But that summer...

I'm certain I experienced another... No, it wasn't just one.

I spent time in several worlds with her—*wishing worlds*.

I remember the propellers of the wind turbines, the beam of the lighthouse, the train track running along the coast, and the pool with its painted walls peeling...

I remember the rusted metal door screeching as it swung open, the age-old beech tree that stood at the fork in the road, and the classroom filled with excited chatter...

Lingering across every one of those scenes is her image.

I see her from behind, as she stares into the ocean, her face as she turns around in the classroom, her practiced form as she swims through the pool—and I remember that moment when she stood in her *yukata* with the setting sun behind her and her eyes transfixed on mine...

I remember her sobbing pleas.

"Norimichi!!"

And I seem to remember distorted scenes, warped sounds, and skewed voices among the wishing worlds I visited that summer.

Her name was Nazuna.

If only... That summer... If only I'd... If only she'd... If only...we could go back to that moment...

The World as It Is

How do bathrooms in old homes manage to start out so incredibly hot and stuffy, right from the beginning of the day?

The bathroom in our house was built underneath our narrow little staircase. Every time you walk in, it feels like the walls are just waiting to squeeze in on you. The bathroom does have one tiny window, but it hardly manages to bring any fresh air inside.

That was how I found myself sitting on the toilet, feeling like a Christmas roast, even though it was the height of summer.

A calendar from a local travel agency hung in front of my face. Its current photo showed a scene of tourists frolicking in the ocean along the coast of Moshimo Beach. The only problem was that Moshimo Beach hadn't seen crowds like that since at least before I was born. I wouldn't have gone so far as to say that the photo was decades and decades old, but I did suspect that it wasn't taken during the current century.

I sighed as I traced the tiny image of a woman in a bright-red, high-legged swimsuit with my finger. I was lost in thought about the babes of another era when I heard rapid knocking at the bathroom door.

"Norimichi!! Hurry up and get out of there!! Dawdling isn't going to change the fact that you've got school today!!"

My mother's hysterics reverberated throughout the tiny room. The already sweltering air seemed to shoot up another three degrees.

Geez. How are moms able to scream that loud first thing in the morning?

I rolled my eyes as I answered, "Leave me alone! I'm not done yet!!"

She seemed to have already walked away without waiting for my response. I heard her call out from the other room, "Breakfast is on the table! It's last night's curry!"

I clutched at my stomach and quietly groaned, "...Come *on*..."

The TV in the living room was reporting on all the big fireworks displays scheduled around the country. I listened as I carefully passed the yolk of a raw egg back and forth between the halves of its broken shell. Once the white had all run off, I plopped the yolk on top of my bowl of curry.

"Eat the white, too! It's good for you!" I felt my mom smack the top of my head with a rolled-up sheaf of newspaper ads. Not a moment later, the room was filled with the blare of the vacuum cleaner.

"Oh, come on. Do you have to do that while I'm eating...?" I wanted to scream each word of my response, but I released them under my breath instead. If I bothered to shout, I'd only get twice the earful back. In a token of defiance, I pointedly left the white untouched and stirred only the yolk into my curry.

Man, if someone manages to invent yolk-only eggs someday, I bet people will buy those things up in droves...

With that thought, I started scooping up mouthfuls using the little scratched-up spoon that had been my favorite since I started elementary school.

Mmm. Delicious!

What was it about curry from the night before that made it so good? There had to be some kind of chemical reaction going on when it sat in its pot overnight or when an egg yolk was mixed in.

"We'll be seeing fireworks all across the nation again tonight! Now, for those of you wondering about the weather…"

The image on the TV switched from a listing of fireworks events to a shot of the weather girl. She stood in front of a map of Japan dotted with an absolutely ridiculous number of little sunshine marks.

The calendar in the bathroom flashed back into mind. Under AUGUST 1 I'd seen the words FIREWORKS DISPLAY… Not that a fireworks display was a *big* deal to me. I mean, I was in seventh grade. But still, it seemed like kind of a special day.

Wait a sec. The weather*'s on? Crap, I gotta get outta here.*

I shoveled the rest of the curry down my throat. When I was finished, I left the bowl on the table and rushed through the door to the storefront. I slipped my sneakers on and tied the laces.

"What a pain… Why do they have us show up for one day in the middle of summer break…?" I grumbled to myself, working my tongue around the inside of my mouth as I tried to pry out a piece of chicken stuck between two molars.

"Consider yourself lucky."

The reply came from my dad, who was cleaning some fishing rods in the shop. He wore a tank top, shorts, and sandals—not exactly the attire you choose when expecting customers.

My family had been running the Shimada Tackle Shop for generations… Or more bluntly, my grandpa had set it up on a whim after he retired as a fisherman. It had been in business for some twenty-odd years, stocking fishing gear along with general household goods, nonperishables, pet food…you know, just about what you'd expect at a tackle shop. Dad took over from Grandpa, but I didn't have any plans to carry on the trade.

"Huh? Why's that?"

"Because *you* don't have t—"

As if she'd timed herself to drown out Dad's words, my mom's voice erupted from the living room. "Norimichi! Put your dishes in the sink when you're done eating! Also, we're heading out in the afternoon, so you're on your own for dinner! Find something to eat in the fridge!"

I'm right here! You don't need to scream!

...is what went through my mind. The words that left my mouth were those of a well-behaved son: "Got it!"

I looked back at my dad, who was still working on the rods.

"You're going somewhere tonight?"

"She's got a bunch of junk she wants to take over to the flea market at Moshimo Shrine."

"The one at the festival? Who's gonna come to *that*?"

"Not to mention it's hardly worth closing the shop for a whole d—"

He stopped himself short and turned back to his work on the rods. Confused, I swiveled my head—only to find Mom standing right behind me.

Her expression was flat. *Now* it was time to be scared.

"...You were saying?" She angled herself toward Dad.

"Well, I'm outta here!!" Sensing trouble brewing, I dashed out of the shop and onto the street outside.

"*Junk*, huh?! Well, if it's so much trouble, you don't have to come!"

An image of my dad anxiously shaking his head back and forth floated to mind as I hopped onto my worn-out bicycle, which was parked just outside the shop. I began pedaling down the sloped road that led to the sea.

I knew I'd probably be drenched in sweat soon, but that brief downhill stretch would bathe my entire body in a cool ocean breeze. It was a treat that left me feeling happy—just a little bit, mind you—to have been born in such a small seaside town.

Moshimo was made up of an old fishing port and a short stretch of coastline. Beyond that was the Pacific Ocean. Moshimo's population was...about 2,800, if I remembered right. Most of its residents lived along the foothills sloping up from the port to the mountains, and the way the houses were built made them look like they were clinging desperately to the mountainside.

"It's like a run-down version of Onomichi. The slow, quiet atmosphere is nice, though." A young tourist from Tokyo had said that about the town. He'd come to Moshimo to do some fishing.

I didn't know much about Onomichi, but it seemed like a pretty rude thing to say. Still, it was hard to argue with the fact that things had slowed down around Moshimo.

Back in the day, we'd been a pretty lively fishing town. And in the summers, tourists used to flock to Moshimo because it was one of the only swimming beaches in the prefecture. But ever since the big earthquake and tsunami six years ago, the town had lost all its pep. Compared with what happened in Tohoku, our damage was minimal, and we were lucky enough not to have any casualties. Even so, the fishing port had been wrecked, and even six years later, it was only half-rebuilt. As for the beaches, only the locals really visited them anymore.

"Man, it feels like you're living in another era when you're here." The tourist from Tokyo had said that, too.

"Another era?" What was that supposed to mean? It didn't seem like he was taking a jab at the town from the way he said it, but at the same time, I'm pretty sure he wasn't about to consider moving in.

If you were to ask me if I liked living in my town, honestly, I wouldn't be able to tell you. I mean, I definitely thought Tokyo sounded like a cool place, but I wasn't sure I'd like to *live* there...

On the other hand, if you were to ask me if I wanted to stay in Moshimo my entire life, I don't think I could get excited about that idea, either.

"Norimichi!!" A voice called out to me.

I turned in its direction and caught sight of a slick new mountain bike flying out from a side road connected to the slope. Riding it was Yusuke Azumi. Yusuke was the son of a doctor, and the two of us basically grew up together. Aside from my parents, I'd bet I'd spent more time with Yusuke than anyone else in my life.

"Yo!"

"'Sup!" I raised a hand from my handlebars as I responded.

As if on cue, two more friends joined us from another side road: Junichi riding his skateboard and Minoru on his kick scooter. As the four of us sped down the slope, our usual morning banter commenced.

"What are the stakes today?"

Junichi was the tallest. His voice had deepened, too. Despite those traits, he didn't act much like an adult, and in fact, among the four of us, he was usually the one making pointless bets. He was also the one most likely to be setting the mood and causing trouble. For Junichi, everything always had to be a competition. Honestly, it was kind of childish. Still, we four had a long-standing, unspoken agreement since elementary school that if a bet was made, we all were immediately on board.

"Whoever loses makes a pass at Ms. Miura!"

Minoru hadn't grown an inch since fourth grade, not to mention any pubes, but he was the one always making edgy, grown-up comments. He tended to act kind of like Junichi's right-hand man. The two were always playing off each other.

"Hey, anyone else think that Ms. Miura's boobs have gotten even bigger over the summer?"

"Did you know that boobs get bigger if you let someone massage 'em?"

"Seriously?!"

"Who's she got massaging her boobs?!"

"Oh man, I wanna try!!"

That was how it usually was for us: talking about nothing particular, half drowned out by the ocean breeze, as we made our way down the last of the slope and onto the road following the coastline.

I glanced back and saw the wind turbines lined up along the mountain ridge, their propellers slowly rotating clockwise.

Wind energy was the city's new initiative. Test projects had begun the year before last. If nothing else, Moshimo had an abundant, stable supply of wind coming in off the ocean, and that apparently made the town an ideal candidate for generating wind energy.

I'd seen that ridgeline a million times since I was a kid. When the turbines first showed up and changed the view, it just hadn't seemed right to me. But over time, I'd grown accustomed to the new residents.

"Shortcut!" Yusuke's mountain bike suddenly veered from the coastal road, down a small stone stairway, and out onto the boardwalk.

"Oh, come on!"

"No fair!"

The rest of us, with our wimpy tires and tiny wheels, were no match for his thick, off-road tires. We had to jump off our own rides and then carry them down the stairs to the boardwalk. At the bottom, we remounted and chased after Yusuke.

I was just getting ready to throw all my weight into the pedals again, when suddenly a strong gust of wind blew past us. As if beckoned, I turned my head to look out at the ocean. My eyes caught sight of an indistinct silhouette near the water's edge.

At first, I assumed it was a particularly energetic sightseer out for a morning stroll. But as my gaze lingered, the figure came into focus, and I saw a white-topped school uniform, a skirt with a hem just above the knee, and long hair in braids.

It was a girl from my class: Nazuna Oikawa.

She was far away, and her back was turned to me, but I was sure of it. It was Nazuna.

Nazuna was lightly stepping across the concrete tetrapod blocks piled along the shore. From where I stood, it almost looked as if she were walking on the surface of the water itself. As she made her way along, the water glittered with the light of the sun behind her. She looked just like a heroine from the movies or on TV.

Time seemed to be moving slowly in the space immediately around her. My eyes were transfixed, and I found myself hoping she might turn my way...

That small, silently held desire was interrupted by a shout from Junichi. "Norimichi! We're gonna be late!!"

Coming back to my senses, I pressed down on my pedals.

"I know!"

I stood up from my seat to pedal harder but took one more look at the shore. Nazuna had crouched down and was picking up something from the shallows. When she had fished it out of the water, she turned toward the sun and held it high in her right hand. Because of the distance, I couldn't tell what the object was.

I had the impression that the glint coming from whatever she'd found was not the same light shimmering on the waves. Or maybe it was just my imagination...

"Heeeey, badda, badda!!"

"Horsehide! Horsehide! Come on, right here!!"

"Bringin' the gas!"

The baseball team—on the field for practice every day of the year except New Year's Eve and New Year's Day—seemed uncharacteristically happy for a school day in the middle of summer.

They were taking up the entire schoolyard, and as they practiced, they shouted all kinds of gibberish at each other.

The rest of the school's students slowly walked by, still in a summer stupor... Of course, the four of us were no exception. We trudged toward the doors of the school building as the warning bell rang out. Our bicycles, board, and scooter had been stashed in the parking lot of a nearby convenience store.

Hearing the baseball team, Junichi mockingly remarked, "What's *badda* supposed to be anyway?"

"A *batter*, I guess?" Minoru responded with a big laugh. "You'd think they could at least pronounce it right."

"Yeah, and what about *horsehide*?"

"Isn't that what they call the ball?"

"And *bringin' the gas*?"

"No clue."

Soccer had been the sport in vogue since we were little, and in comparison, baseball seemed well past its prime. As far as we were concerned, baseball was for old farts. But because Moshimo's vocational school had once won the national high school championships, baseball had been slow to wane here, and plenty of kids in the town preferred it to soccer.

A wayward ball rolled toward our feet, and a dirt-smeared member of the team chased it down at full speed.

"I can't believe the whole team's still got buzz cuts. You'd think that kind of thing would have died out years ago."

"Never gonna score with a girl looking like *that*."

"I can't even imagine why anyone would sign up for baseball."

We scoffed, but actually, Yusuke, Junichi, Minoru, and I had all been on a little league team during our first three years of elementary. Our parents had made us. We were completely uninterested, and instead of practicing, we'd kick the rubber kiddie baseballs around on the ground like soccer balls. Eventually, the coach got fed up and declared that we had all "voluntarily" retired ourselves from the team. We four had been friends before then, but the little league fiasco was what really brought us close.

No single member of our group stood out as the leader, but Junichi was usually the one starting games and conversations, and Minoru was quick to follow along. When it came to topics, though, Junichi seemed to be eternally stuck in elementary school. Recently, Yusuke and I had begun to get a little tired of it.

"Pick up the pace, guys!!"

A bright voice echoed out behind us, and we turned to see Ms. Miura riding up from the school gates on a granny bike. Her chest bobbed as she pedaled, and the buttons running down her white blouse looked about ready to pop off.

"Oh man, we've got some serious action again today."

"I'd say that's about a six on the Richter scale."

"Who came in last?"

"Junichi!"

"Oh yeah, like a skateboard's gonna beat a bike!"

Even as he complained, Junichi sprinted forward with a big grin on his face. A moment later, he was jumping onto the back of Ms. Miura's bicycle.

"Hey! Get off of there!"

Ms. Miura's handlebars wobbled unsteadily from the sudden extra weight. Junichi's hands reached around and firmly gripped the woman's chest.

"That is *not* appropriate!"

Ms. Miura slammed on her brakes and then threw her elbows back. Junichi avoided the blow, hopped off the bicycle, and started running across the schoolyard.

"Tajima! You get back here *this instant*!!"

As she sped after him on her bike, the remaining three of us broke down laughing and called out, "Junichi! How big are they?!"

"J-J-J-J-J-J-J-J-J cup!!"

He held up his hands in the shape of a J. As he continued to run, he passed in front of a girl walking toward the school building.

It was Nazuna.

"There's no way they're *that* big!!"

Junichi and Ms. Miura had sped right in front of Nazuna's eyes, but the girl hadn't even turned her head. She'd continued walking straight forward, unfazed and uninterested. It might have been my imagination, but the expression on Nazuna's face seemed a little sad.

Something felt different about her…first the strange behavior along the coastline that morning and now that melancholy expression. My musings, however, were soon drowned out by the ringing of the school bell.

The classroom bustled with the happy, awkward reunions unique to a day at school after a break.

Nazuna's seat was precisely in the middle of the room. A chubby girl one seat back was talking to her.

"Hey, Nazuna. Have you been anywhere for summer break?"

"Not yet."

"I'm going to Disneyland next week!"

"Oh, that sounds great."

"Have you been anywhere?" Right. It was pretty clear she'd only bothered to ask so she'd have an opening to brag about her Disneyland trip.

Nazuna smiled as she talked, seeming no different from usual. What was the reason for that strange unease I'd felt earlier?

I sat in my seat at the back of the classroom, in the row next to the windows. I'd spent the entire first term of school gazing at Nazuna from that desk. Most of the time, I was only seeing her from behind, but every once in a while, when she was passing papers back, or—like now—when someone behind her struck up a conversation, I'd catch a glimpse of Nazuna turned around in her seat. Every time it happened, I'd find myself awestruck... When had she become so alluring?

Nazuna had moved here from Tokyo when we were in fifth grade. I could tell immediately that she was different from any of the girls I'd known growing up in Moshimo.

I'd been just a kid—or, well, I guess I still was a kid—but anyway, even though I knew Nazuna was different, I couldn't quite pin down why. She seemed so sophisticated. So refined. When she was in her school uniform—or even in her gym clothes—she had an aura about her... None of the other girls even compared. When we began junior high and she started growing taller, every extra inch seemed to be accompanied by...

Ugh! Where is all this mushy, lovey-dovey crap coming from?!

But...she was *so* cute...

"Man, she's cute, isn't she? Nazuna Oikawa, I mean."

"Huh?!"

Yusuke's words caught me off guard, and my voice squeaked. Yusuke's seat was directly in front of mine.

"Whoa there, Squeaks."

Yusuke's jab came lightning quick. Eager to avoid any suspicion of interest in the girl, I parried back with my own improvised joke.

"Nazuna? I guess she is fairly...s*nazz*y."

"...Weak."

I tried to act casual. "What's so cute about her anyway?"

"I *really* wanna ask her out."

"Then do it."

Since we'd started junior high, Yusuke had become blatantly more aware of Nazuna.

A while ago, I'd learned that he was quietly snapping pictures of her on his smartphone. The photos were all collected into a folder, and Yusuke couldn't fall asleep at night without scrolling through them. It kind of grossed me out when he told me, but at the same time, I really wanted a copy of that folder.

"I mean, I just wanna go somewhere with her before summer's over. Like the fireworks display tonight…"

"Then you should *ask* her."

"I can't just go up to her like that! What if she says no?!"

"Figure it out!"

"Hey. How 'bout you go ask her for me?"

"Oh yeah, sure… 'Hey, Nazuna, Yusuke has something he wants me to tell you…'"

"'Oh? What's that?'"

"'He says you're the ugliest girl on the planet.'"

"Hey! That's not what I said!"

"That's all, folks! Thanks for watching!"

That had been our standby bit for the last several months. Just as we reached the ending beat, Ms. Miura walked into the classroom.

"In your seats, people!!" Our impatient teacher didn't bother to wait for the scattered students to follow her instructions. She just continued speaking. "All right. Today's the day of the big festival and fireworks display at Moshimo Shrine. There's probably going to be some pretty big crowds. I want you all to be careful and not to stay out too late—especially those of you going with friends."

Minoru shot up out of his seat as if he'd been waiting all morning for this opportunity. "Ms. Miura, who are *you* going to the festival with?"

Aside from being impatient, Ms. Miura was also a terrible liar.

"Um…" No sooner had she faltered than the classroom erupted in excited chatter.

Junichi struck the coup de grâce. "I bet you're going with your *boyfriend*, right? And after the show's over, maybe you're planning a grand finale of your own at a hotel?!"

"*Tajima!* You better learn to control yourself, or you're going to be on the receiving end of a harassment lawsuit!"

"Then I'll just countersue for abuse of power!"

"You are simply *unbelievable*, you know that?" Ms. Miura began making her way from her desk toward Junichi. Her chest bounced with her sudden, sharp movements.

"Ms. Miura! Do you have a license to be carrying around fireworks like that?!"

"Junichi Tajima!!"

Laughter enveloped the entire classroom, and Ms. Miura and Junichi began a chaotic game of tag.

Looks like somebody's parents will be making another after-school visit... I shook my head. As my eyes loosely followed the unremarkable scene, I caught sight of Nazuna again. She was facing toward me.

Huh...?

No, she wasn't just turned my way... Her gaze was locked *directly on me...*

I'd spent the whole term stealing glances, but that was the first time our eyes had ever met.

Nazuna knew I was returning her gaze. Her face was blank, but something deep in her eyes seemed to be reaching out to me—pleading with me.

The connection lasted only an instant... Within a second or two, our eyes had broken away.

She turned to face forward in her seat while I continued staring in confusion at her back. She didn't turn around again.

"Junichi! Your mother is going to be hearing from me!!"

I was about to shift my attention back to the usual ruckus between Ms. Miura and Junichi. That's when I saw it: a strange light in the corner of my eye. A quilted bag hung from a hook at the side of Nazuna's desk. The bottom of the bag seemed to be shrouded in a strange halo.

No, not shrouded... It was more like something inside was faintly shining through the fabric...

What is that...?

I felt as if I were being pulled in toward the light. I couldn't turn away. Just then, Junichi and Ms. Miura blocked my view and brought me back to my senses. Ms. Miura had finally caught the boy right in front of my desk.

"Nooo! Have mercy! Norimichiii, help meee!"

Ms. Miura gave Junichi a light tap on the top of his head. The room's laughter peaked, and the go-to comedy routine of first-year Class 1-C came to an end.

As Junichi was led back to his seat by the scruff of his neck, I stole another glance at Nazuna's bag. The light was gone.

A loud *screeeech* rang through the outside summer air. Beyond the rusted iron gate, a staircase rose up before us. The stairs had once been light blue, but most of their paint had since peeled away. We vaulted the steps two at a time, and at the top we found clear blue sky, lounging white clouds, and a spread of green forest. The same beautiful scenery was re-created in the still water of a twenty-five-meter pool before Yusuke and me.

Yusuke tossed the mop he'd been holding to the side and said, "Whaddaya think? Shall we ditch the cleaning?"

"Don't you know? Pool cleaning duty comes with a special perk. Since the swim team already cleans the pool every day, there's really nothing for us to do!" I replied.

"Sounds about right."

Yusuke and I grinned from ear to ear: We had the entire pool to ourselves. We stripped off our gym clothes and pulled tight the waist cords on our school-issued (and decidedly unfashionable) athletic trunks. With goggles strapped to our heads and shoes tossed aside, we started our dash to the pool—only to stop short.

"Ow!"

"Geez! My feet are gonna burn off!"

The concrete poolside had been subject to its own bath of scorching sun all morning long. It would have been easier to walk our bare feet across hot coals.

"Oh man... Let's just jump in alrea— Huh?"

Yusuke cut himself off. I looked up and found him staring over my shoulder.

"Nazuna?" he said.

I followed his gaze to the other side of the pool.

"Oh..."

There, twenty-five meters away, sitting atop the starting blocks and wearing her athletic one-piece swimsuit, was Nazuna.

My eyes were unconsciously drawn to her faintly swelling chest. They continued downward, along the gentle curves that connected her rounded hips to her thighs and firm calves. Nazuna's feet dangled in the pool. She slowly dragged them back and forth through the water, creating ripples that distorted her reflected self.

"Um...was she on pool duty today?"

"Pretty sure it's just the two of us."

"Oh, is she on the swim team, then...? Do they have practice today?"

"No idea."

"Hey, I gotta go to the bathroom."

"Huh? Why?"

"Dunno. Saw Nazuna, and now I gotta take a dump." No sooner were the words out of his mouth than Yusuke started waddling away with his arms and legs held stiff.

"You're *so* weird."

It was an old quirk of Yusuke's. Ever since we were in kindergarten, any time something unexpected confronted him, he'd suddenly need to go.

One time, we were in the middle of a soccer game. He'd been

fouled and was lined up to make his penalty kick. The ref's whistle sounded, and Yusuke just shot off the field toward the restrooms.

I shifted my gaze from Yusuke's awkward waddle back to Nazuna…

Huh? What in the world is she doing?

Now she was lying faceup, as if the poolside were her bed. The rays of the hot summer sun beat down on her. I was alone at the pool with Nazuna. A cacophony of morning cicadas served only to underscore the awkward quiet between us.

Is she waiting for something? What am I supposed to do in a situation like this?

It felt ridiculous to just stand there waiting for Yusuke to get back. And Nazuna had to have noticed I was there. It would be decidedly uncool for me to just hang around uncomfortably on my side of the pool…

Mentally arming myself with that slew of excuses, I moved closer to Nazuna. When I was about six feet away, I could see her expression. She was lying with her eyes closed and her mouth fixed into a faint smile, which made her somehow feel further away than she actually was. I sensed I shouldn't get any closer to her and stopped walking.

"…Um… Out sunbathing today?"

My words came out much quieter than expected, but Nazuna seemed to hear them. She shook her head slightly from one side to the other.

I forced an awkward cough and then asked, "Um, got practice today?"

"…Nope."

"Um… Just going for a swim?"

"Not swimming."

"Uhh… Why are you here, then?"

"Guess."

"…I have no idea."

Nazuna's eyes stayed closed throughout the exchange.

"Why, oh why, could I be here?"

"..."

It felt like we were in the middle of some kind of avant-garde comedy sketch. I'm a straightforward guy: setup and payoff. I didn't think I could go on like that, so I just stopped responding. How was *I* supposed to know why she was there? Without the faintest idea what kind of response she was fishing for, all I could do was shut up and listen to the background music, compliments of the Moshimo Cicada Chamber Choir.

A dragonfly bobbed languidly before my eyes. It briefly touched down on the surface of the pool two or three times, then doubled back and began circling just above Nazuna. Finally, it perched...right on one of the shoulder straps of Nazuna's swimsuit.

Nazuna didn't so much as flinch. It was impossible to tell whether she was aware of the dragonfly or not.

"Hey."

"Yeah?"

"It landed on you."

"What did?"

"A white-tailed dragonfly."

"...Grab it."

"Huh?"

"Catch it."

Nazuna continued to speak to me with her eyes closed. Her tone was hard to place. It might have been the cute pleading of a smitten girl, or it could have been the listless teasing of someone well aware they had the upper hand...

Dragonfly catching wasn't anything new to me. But the dragonfly's location was...problematic. I hesitantly drew nearer, and soon my vision was entirely filled with Nazuna's supine figure. The fact took me more by surprise than it ought to have.

When we did swimming in PE, girls and boys were always

split into separate classes. This was the first time I'd ever seen a girl in a swimsuit up close. The whole situation seemed kind of suggestive...

Whoa, there! Keep your mind on the task at hand! And man, would the cicadas just shut up already?!

I turned my head to one side, trying to angle it away from Nazuna as I leaned in and reached toward her collarbone. My valiant attempt to look away predictably faltered when I realized my eyes were now pointed directly at her breast. My hand started to quaver.

The dragonfly! Focus on the dragonfly!

I repeated my newfound mantra and continued to stretch out my hand. My thumb and index finger were a quarter inch apart, closing in on the dragonfly's wing...

The dragonfly sprang into the air.

"Oh..."

I followed the insect's course high up into the sky. Nazuna sat up.

"You're pretty bad at that."

She looked at my dumbfounded face as I stared up at the dragonfly, and she laughed at me.

"Am not!"

I glanced down at her face but received an eyeful of cleavage, too. Embarrassed, I turned away. It was probably the first time I'd talked face-to-face with Nazuna since we started junior high.

There was a small, round object lying at Nazuna's feet. It looked like some kind of stone...or ball...or maybe an orb.

It was perfectly round—too round to have been formed by nature—and its surface was etched with a mysterious, ineffable pattern.

"Hey... What's that?"

"Huh? Oh, this...? I found it in the ocean earlier today."

Nazuna scooped up the mysterious orb and handed it to me.

So this is what I saw her fishing out of the ocean before school...

It was about the size of a tennis ball, and though it had looked fairly large while in Nazuna's hand, it seemed a bit smaller in mine. Its weight seemed both too heavy and yet too light for something of its size and build. The texture was unlike anything I'd held before.

"Is it a rock? ...Or made of some kind of glass?"

"I don't know. I picked it up because I thought it looked pretty."

"It's really weird..."

I held the orb up in the sunlight. The strange hues covering its surface grew more intense. I didn't disagree with Nazuna. It was quite pretty.

We stayed like that for a moment, both admiring the orb held in my hand, until a loud *clang* rang out from the iron gate at the pool's entrance. I shoved the orb back into Nazuna's hand and hurriedly made my way back to the other side of the pool.

On the way, I stole one more glance at Nazuna. She was looking intently at the orb in her hand.

Yusuke returned to the pool with a strangely satisfied expression. He announced happily, "Nothing came out!"

"Um... Okay?"

Then, what are you looking so smug about? I wanted to prod, but I hadn't yet recovered from my encounter with Nazuna.

"Why, oh why, could I be here?" Her words crossed through my mind again.

I was obviously agitated, but Yusuke seemed to pay no mind. He wrapped an arm around my shoulders.

"More importantly, I just had a great idea."

"What's that?"

"Wanna race? Two laps of the pool. Let's place a bet on it."

"Sounds great!"

What was so "great" about the idea and what it was "more

important" than, I had no idea. I was ready to jump on any suggestion, if it meant keeping the conversation away from Nazuna. I pulled my goggles down over my eyes and climbed up on one of the starting blocks.

"All right. If I win…you gotta buy me the newest issue of *One Piece*," I said to Yusuke.

"Hah! Sounds good!"

"What about you?"

"If I win…I'm gonna ask out Nazuna."

"Huh?!"

No sooner was the sound out of my mouth than Yusuke had taken a head start, diving into the pool.

I panicked and shouted out, "Hey! What gives, man?! No fair!"

Yusuke continued to swim for about fifteen feet, then stopped and lifted his head out of the water. "Can't take a joke? I know you want Nazuna for yourself."

I froze. My heart gave one big *thump!* Had Yusuke even gone to the bathroom at all? Maybe he'd been standing there the whole time, watching everything that happened between Nazuna and me.

"What? What are you talking about?" I protested.

"You and Nazuna. You were talking just now, weren't you?"

Yusuke climbed back up onto his starting block. I could feel the intensity of his glare despite his goggles. His eyes dug into me.

"No. I didn't say anything to her…"

"You like her, too, don't you?"

"Huh? Where'd you get that from?"

"…"

"…"

We stood locked in a brief, icy silence until a strangely sunny voice broke through.

"You guys racing?"

The pitter-patter of Nazuna's feet echoed out as she jogged toward us.

Unconcerned by our lack of response, she began climbing onto a starting block beside us and said, "I'm in."

"What? Um, sorry, this is between Yusuke and me. Right?"

"Uh, yeah. Just us."

She stood atop the block now, acting as if she hadn't heard us. "What's the bet?"

"Um, well..."

One Piece aside, we sure weren't in any hurry to tell her about Yusuke's bet. But what had shocked me the most was the sweeping change in Nazuna's expression and voice. It was like she was a completely different person from the one I'd been talking to just moments before.

"Well, if *I* win, you have to do whatever I say."

"What kind of bet is that?!"

"Come on! Whatever I say, okay?"

"...Okay... I guess."

"...All right."

Yusuke and I were still unconvinced. *"Whatever I say?"* There were way too many possibilities. But it was clear Nazuna wasn't going to budge. We gave in to her frivolous terms.

"All right. Ready...!"

Nazuna leaned forward on her block. She was clearly an experienced swimmer.

What was going on? How had we put ourselves in this situation? Yusuke and I exchanged dumbfounded looks, but when Nazuna called out "Set...!" we each scrambled into position.

"Go!"

The three of us plunged into the water.

Based on the arc of our dives, Nazuna was already in the lead. Under the surface, I could see her practiced form. She was pulling farther and farther ahead. Yusuke and I, on the other hand, were neck and neck. I pulled myself through the water with all my might.

Nazuna had a good fifteen-foot lead on us when she spun in the water and kicked against the far wall. It was a flawless turn. She sailed back toward us through a wall of bubbles. Her braids swayed behind her.

As Nazuna and I passed each other, our eyes met.

It was the third time that day: first in the classroom, then poolside, and now here. Each time, the eyes—and the things they made me feel—had been completely different. This time, too, I felt her eyes trying to tell me something. I didn't know what it was, and I couldn't explain how I knew they were. I just did.

At that moment, it occurred to me why I could see her eyes so clearly.

Huh? She swims without goggles…?

Maybe it happened because I'd let my mind wander from the race, but when I went in for the turn, my body wasn't ready. My foot was at a weird angle, and by the time I realized what was about to happen, it was too late.

Slam!

"Ow!"

Right at the turn, my foot had shot out of the water and come smashing down against the lip of the pool. I felt pain surge through my ankle. While I flailed about in the water, I saw the shape of Nazuna—and Yusuke, too—recede into the distance.

Amid the bubbles bursting before my eyes, I caught sight of something else. The orb that Nazuna had been staring at so intently was sinking through the water, headed to the bottom of the pool. Nazuna must have left it at the edge of the pool, and the shock from my ankle had caused it to roll in.

I instinctively reached out to it. The orb stopped its descent.

"?"

It hadn't just stopped sinking. It was now slowly spinning in the water and wavering slightly. It began to emit a faint ray of light that stretched outward like the beam from a lighthouse and cast a spotlight along the walls of the pool.

The world seemed to be moving in slow motion. The orb resumed its descent ever so gradually, as if serenely allowing itself to sink.

"???"

What on earth was happening...? Was it some sort of illusion caused by the sunlight reflecting off the orb in the water?

My hand continued to reach out, and finally, I grasped the strange object. The light it had been emitting immediately vanished.

At the same moment, I realized just how long I'd been holding my breath. I struggled up to the surface for air. Nazuna and Yusuke had both finished swimming. I saw them at the other end of the pool talking about something.

He wasn't *really* asking her out, was he?

With the orb still in hand, I resumed my crawl to the other end of the pool. I managed to make it back to the starting side and brought my head out of the water. Nazuna was standing at the side of the pool and staring at me with water still streaming down her face. I looked around, wondering where Yusuke was, and found him slowly sinking under the surface. Bunches of air bubbles burbled up from the empty expression on his face.

"Hey!"

I splashed over to try to bring Yusuke back to the surface. As I flailed my arms, I realized that the orb was still in my hand. Nazuna must have noticed it, too, and her hand shot out in my direction.

"Give it back."

"Huh?"

For a second, I didn't understand what she meant.

She repeated herself more forcefully. "That. It's mine."

Her insistence caught me off guard. Of course I knew the orb was hers. She'd been showing it to me just a few minutes ago. Was it that important to her?

The whole exchange struck me as unusual, but I plopped the orb down into her outstretched hand. The orb safely recovered, Nazuna began walking toward the pool's exit, without so much as a glance back.

I watched her departing figure from the water.

First, there was the awkward comedy sketch, and after that came the perplexing fifty-meter race in the pool. What on earth was Nazuna trying to accomplish?

The bell rang, signaling that the school day was over. We'd managed to spend our entire time on cleaning duty at the pool without actually cleaning an inch. Yusuke and I made our way back to the classroom. He was silent as we walked through the hallways.

"Hey."

"Yeah?"

"Something happen to you?"

"Huh? What do you mean?"

Yusuke was definitely acting fishy. Ever since that moment he'd shared with Nazuna at the side of the pool, he'd been distracted by something. I mustered up all my courage and spelled out what I really wanted to ask.

"Back there at the pool. Did you ask Nazuna out?"

"Huh?! What are you talking about?! Why would I ever do that?! Don't be stupid!" He brushed me off, then shuffled ahead.

"I— Never mind… Sorry."

Why was he acting pissed off all of a sudden? I was feeling pretty fed up with Yusuke but continued to follow him back to the classroom.

When we arrived, Junichi and Minoru were having some kind of argument with Kazuhiro in front of the blackboard.

"They're round!" Kazuhiro's shrill voice reverberated throughout the room.

Kazuhiro was the best student in the class. As serious as he was about studying, he quickly became riled up any time there was an argument.

"No, they're not. They're flat. What are you, stupid?" Junichi took every chance he saw to get a rise out of Kazuhiro, and he prodded teasingly with his reply.

"I'm telling you, they're round! Think about it! The powder inside ignites, and then it explodes outward in all directions. Of course they're going to be round!"

"Hey, Norimichi. If you see a firework explode from the side, does it still look round like a globe, or is it flat like a pancake?"

Junichi had noticed us walk into the room. He was eager to drag us into the conversation, but his question confronted me so suddenly, I struggled to respond.

"What do you mean? Like a bottle rocket?" I ended up stalling.

Minoru, obviously on Junichi's side, chimed in. "No! Big ones, like at a fireworks display! Like the kind they'll be using at the show tonight!"

"Display fireworks? Um…flat, I guess?"

I wasn't very invested in my answer, but Junichi proclaimed his victory with a few more vocal jabs at Kazuhiro.

"See?"

"Don't be ridiculous! They're totally round!!"

"Yusuke? What do you think?"

Yusuke, who had returned to his seat and was putting on his backpack, replied with a complete lack of interest. "Huh? I dunno."

As if triggered by Yusuke's lackadaisical response, Kazuhiro's speech grew more and more heated. "Are you all stupid?! Have you ever seen a sparkler before? Round, right?!"

"Just because sparklers are round doesn't mean the big ones are the same!" Junichi's voice had risen, too.

"All right, so have any of you ever seen a flat firework before?!"

"I have!" Minoru stood in front of Kazuhiro, full of confidence as he stared up Kazuhiro's extra foot of height. "Last year, I watched the fireworks display from my grandpa's yard. The fireworks were totally flat. Grandpa said it was because his house is at a bad angle for viewing the show."

"See! If his grandpa says so, it has to be true!"

"His grandpa's off his rocker!"

"No, he's not! Not all the way anyway!"

"This conversation is going nowhere," Kazuhiro declared, exasperated.

"Then, let's take a vote!" Junichi charged.

"It's not something you vote about! Fireworks are round, and that's that!!"

"Anyone who thinks they're flat, raise your hand!"

Oh, come on. This conversation is ridiculous.

By now, I'd gotten the gist of it: Would fireworks in the sky at a professional show always look round, no matter where you were standing? Or was that roundness dependent on the angle you were watching from? It seemed like Junichi, Minoru, and Kazuhiro had been at it for some time.

Personally, I was more concerned about my ankle, which had begun to ache. I wanted to go home already.

I turned my attention away from the silly vote to find Nazuna walking into the classroom. She'd changed back into her uniform.

Nazuna walked straight to her desk. This time, rather than shooting a glance in my direction, she looked at Yusuke instead. Their eyes met, and Nazuna kept her gaze firmly fixed. Yusuke appeared to grow uncomfortable, and he turned away to look out the windows.

It seemed like something *had* happened at the pool, after all...

As I was trying to piece it together, Nazuna wordlessly picked up her school bag and headed out the classroom door. Just before she disappeared down the hallway, she glanced back one more time. It was hard to tell whether she was looking at Yusuke or me.

She hadn't bothered to close the door behind her. My eyes lingered there for a while.

"All right. If you're *that* sure, let's make a bet."

Kazuhiro's words, suddenly calm, pulled me back to reality.

"Hah! Okay. And if fireworks *are* flat, you've gotta do our summer homework. All of it—for all four of us."

I didn't really care about the fireworks, but those last words out of Junichi's mouth caught my attention.

"Yeah!" I chimed in. "That's our bet!!"

I was reminded that I hadn't even touched my summer homework yet. The ridiculous argument suddenly seemed a lot more important.

"Okay. And if they're round?"

"I'll give you an up-skirt pic of Ms. Miura!" As Junichi made his latest announcement, he held his smartphone up alongside his face.

It was common knowledge in the class that Kazuhiro had a thing for Ms. Miura.

"What?! You've got a picture like that?!"

"Nah. I'll take it for ya."

"How?"

"I'll just bend over like I dropped something, angle the camera like so, and *snap!*"

Junichi struck a pose, leaning backward as if he were about to do the limbo, then mimicked the shutter noise of a camera.

As I watched, unimpressed, another thought occurred to me. "...Hey, how do you plan on seeing a firework from the side anyway?"

"That's easy."

Kazuhiro walked over to a map of Moshimo affixed to one of the classroom's walls.

"See here? Moshimo Lighthouse is right to the side."

Most of the spectators for the fireworks display that night would be lined up along the crescent-shaped Moshimo Beach. The beach skirted the edge of a bay, which had a small island precisely in the middle. The fireworks were always launched from that island.

"The fireworks shoot up from Moshimo Island," Kazuhiro continued. "And that means we can see the fireworks from the side if we're standing there, right?"

As if to seal his victory, Kazuhiro brought a finger up to the bridge of his nose and coolly adjusted his glasses.

Not to be outdone by Kazuhiro's sudden logical insight, Junichi doubled down with a firm response. "Perfect! So we're all going to the lighthouse tonight, yeah?!!"

"Huh? All of us?"

I'd played along with Junichi's bet, but actually going to the lighthouse was another story. It wasn't just some short walk. The local schools held an annual 10K run in the winter, and the course used the road that led up to the lighthouse. The agony of past runs flooded my mind, but there was no stopping Junichi now.

"What do you mean? Of course we're all going. Yusuke, you're coming, too, right?"

Yusuke, who had been all but uninvolved up until now, blinked in surprise at the sudden inquiry. "Huh? Where?"

"To the lighthouse! Oh my gosh! Were you even listening?!?!"

"We're gonna see for ourselves whether fireworks are round or flat and settle this once and for all!"

Overwhelmed by Junichi's and Kazuhiro's gusto, Yusuke scrambled. "Yeah, okay. I'm going."

"Awesome! Okay, so we all meet at Moshimo Shrine at five PM!! No homework all summer. This is gonna be great!!"

"Not likely! And you better be serious about that up-skirt pic!"

Junichi and Minoru gave each other a high five, ignoring Kazuhiro altogether now.

"If it means he does all our homework, I guess it's worth it...," Yusuke mumbled with an uninterested expression on his face as he stared out at the schoolyard.

"Yusuke? What's up?"

"Nothing! Geez, mind your own business."

"Huh? What's got you all pissed off?"

"I'm not pissed off! Okay, let's go to the lighthouse, then! Great!! Sounds like an awesome plan!!"

"Um... Okay..."

Yusuke filed out the door after Junichi and the others, who were still chattering excitedly. I lingered behind, bewildered by Yusuke's sudden shift from snippy to gung ho. What was going on with him...? I glanced out the window he'd been facing. The baseball club was practicing again in the schoolyard. Walking right through the center of the practice was Nazuna. She moved with purpose, as if she'd made up her mind about some plan.

"Five o'clock! You guys better not be late!"

Yusuke raised one hand into the air as he pedaled his mountain bike to the right at the fork in the road. His voice was overly cheerful.

"Huh? What's got him so happy?"

"No idea... A while ago he was telling me all about how he couldn't take a dump, though."

"Ah, so he's got a bunch of extra fuel packed up inside, then."

Junichi, Minoru, and I held our low-IQ conversation under the shade of the age-old beech tree standing between the two diverging paths. We watched as Yusuke receded into the distance.

A rusted old noticeboard stood in front of the tree. The town had affixed a poster there that read:

LIGHT OF HOPE

AUGUST 1

MOSHIMO FIREWORKS DISPLAY

7 PM TO 8 PM

The background of the poster was filled with photos of multi-colored firework explosions. It was the same design they used every year.

"Um, don't the fireworks on here look pretty round to you…?" Minoru asked worriedly, an ice pop hanging out of the corner of his mouth.

Junichi answered reassuringly, "That's just 'cause they shot the pictures from the front. If you look at it from the side like this… See? Totally flat!"

Junichi stood to the side of the noticeboard and stared at the poster with one eye shut.

Minoru followed his lead, then announced, "You're right!"

"See? Why are we even bothering with the lighthouse? …Huh? Hey, Norimichi, you're bleeding."

"I am?"

I followed Junichi's eyes down to my feet. One white sock was tinged red with blood.

"Oh yeah… Earlier at the pool, I was making a turn and smashed my ankle."

"On a turn? Smooth."

"My foot just shot out farther than I expected."

"How does something like that even happen?"

"I dunno."

As I related the story of my ankle to Junichi, I was confronted by the mental image of Nazuna's face with her eyes fixed directly on mine as we both swam in the water. Nazuna and I had probably only been looking at each other like that for a second or two, but her gaze had been so intense, it felt much longer.

"Hey, Junichi. Can you keep your eyes open underwater?"

"Huh? You mean without goggles?"

"Yeah."

"No way. It stings."

"Right? Minoru, what about you?"

"I used to be able to. A long time ago, in elementary. Don't you remember? In swimming class, we used to make each other play rock-paper-scissors underwater."

"Oh yeah. I forgot about that."

He was right. When we'd first been learning how to swim and still couldn't do much beyond sticking our heads under the water, we'd have little competitions—like who could grab the chlorine tablet from the bottom of the pool after the teacher had tossed it in.

We hadn't been wearing goggles then, but we'd been able to see everything under the surface clearly.

"Anyway, see you at five, right?"

"Yeah."

Junichi and Minoru rode their skateboard and scooter up the left fork. I watched them go, then lifted my foot up to the pedal of my bike. The dull ache of my ankle changed into a fresh, biting pain. I clenched my teeth and thought again about everything that had happened at the pool.

Did this mean Nazuna was still able to see everything under the surface with perfect clarity?

A makeshift sign reading CLOSED FOR TODAY fluttered in the wind. I circled around behind the shop and pulled our spare house key out from the mailbox. When I opened the door, I was met with the muggy air of a house left unoccupied during a summer day.

"Why does it have to be so hot?"

I threw my sweat-soaked button-down shirt into the laundry basket, then walked into the kitchen. I opened the fridge, expecting to see my half-finished bottle of cola from the day before. It was gone.

Huh? Did Mom throw it away?

I pulled open the freezer and saw a box of my dad's favorite ice pops: Watermelon Bars. There was only one left in the box, and I decided to take it. Whoever came up with the idea of an ice pop that looks just like a wedge of cut watermelon, with an easy-to-eat triangular shape and little chocolate "seeds" inside, was a genius.

The pain in my right ankle had grown a little more intense. I dragged it along the floor and limped up the stairs toward my room. When I threw open the door, Yusuke was sitting there playing *Mario Kart*.

"Whoa!! You scared me!!!"

"Welcome home."

I was so surprised, I'd almost dropped my Watermelon Bar. Yusuke, in contrast, sat calmly playing the game and drinking a bottle of cola—*my* bottle of cola. He didn't even glance in my direction.

"What do you mean, 'Welcome home'? Why are you even here?"

"You guys gotta take better precautions. You can't just leave a spare key in the mailbox. Anybody could find it."

"That doesn't mean you can just waltz right in, you know. And that cola you're drinking is mine."

"Come on, it's no big deal. You're free until five anyway, right? And Hey, so am I!"

"Don't change the subject."

As I gave my last quip, I sat down beside Yusuke. His eyes gleamed at my frozen treat.

"Oh man, a Watermelon Bar. Hey, get me one of those, too."

"Too bad. Last one."

"Haven't you ever heard of a little something called *hospitality*?" With a devilish grin and his controller still in hand, he leaned over and took a bite out of the ice pop.

"Man, whoever came up with the idea of an ice pop shaped like a piece of watermelon was a genius," he continued.

It was these kinds of exchanges that reminded me why we were best friends. Even after some kind of argument or fight, the next time we saw each other, things were back to normal—as if the disagreement had never happened.

I picked up the second controller, and Yusuke switched to two-player mode. He picked Bowser; I picked Luigi. That, too, was how it always was for us.

We'd been so wrapped up in the game, we hardly noticed as the cries of the morning cicadas faded into those of the dusk cicadas.

"Hey, it's almost five."

"No big deal if we're not exactly on time," Yusuke responded as his Bowser drifted around a corner.

"Really? Weren't you the one going on about how we shouldn't be late?"

"Seriously, though. Of course fireworks are round," Yusuke half laughed as he downed the last of his drink.

"Huh? Really?"

"Yeah! Wait a second, you don't really think…?"

"No! I mean, I guess so…," I faltered.

"Are you stupid? In what kind of world do they have flat fireworks? Think about it. There's a bunch of powder inside, and it explodes outward. Of course they're gonna look round, no matter what direction you see them from!"

Yusuke picked up a soccer ball that had been lying in my room and handed it to me. I turned it over in my hands. His explanation definitely seemed logical, but part of me was still unconvinced.

"Yeah, but…what about in comic books? If there's a drawing of a soccer ball in a comic book, it's flat, right…?"

"Well, duh! That's because it's in a *comic*! You know, it's two-dimensional or whatever."

"What're you gonna do if we find out they're flat, though?"

Yusuke met my persistence with an air of exhaustion. "Impossible. There isn't a world where that can happen."

"Then why didn't you say so when they were talking about it at school?"

"Huh? I was just going along with whatever they wanted."

"Really…?"

"Anyway, I guess we should get going. Ugh, what a pain," he said as he stood and hit the power on the console.

Yusuke's mood seemed to be all over the place that day. I was having trouble following the constant ups and downs. At any rate, we both headed to the back door.

"Ouch…"

When I tried to put on my sneakers, my right foot wouldn't fit in its shoe. I looked at my ankle more closely. The blood had stopped, but the area around the wound was now swollen. The most disconcerting thing was the appearance of the wound itself. It was so weird and squishy I could hardly bear to keep my eyes on it.

When Yusuke looked over, he let out a big yelp.

"Ew! What happened?! Gross!"

"It's from when I smashed it at the pool, remember?"

"At the pool? You hit your ankle?"

"You were there! When we were racing!"

"Huh? Racing? What are you talking about?"

"Come on. You, me, and Oikawa. We had a fifty-meter race."

"Where are you getting this from?"

I couldn't tell if he was playing dumb or if he'd actually forgotten. He looked completely serious, and it left me feeling unsure of myself. I didn't press the issue any further.

"Anyway, you should see a doctor about that."

"It's no big deal."

"You don't know that. If you contract tetanus, you could die."

"…Really?"

I didn't necessarily believe Yusuke just because his dad was a doctor… More that something in his voice seemed really convincing. It was making me nervous.

"Go to my place and ask my dad to take a look. I'll let Junichi and the others know."

"Huh? No way. Come with me. And…I don't have any money anyway."

"If I go with you, we'll both be late, and they'll wonder where we are. Just go. You can pay for it later."

It occurred to me that he'd changed his position again about whether it was okay to be late. However, I didn't want to risk a serious disease. I was starting to think that I ought to go and have my ankle checked out, after all.

As if he'd sensed my feelings, Yusuke put an arm around my shoulder. His voice softened.

"One more thing."

"What?"

"If Nazuna's at my house, tell her that I won't be able to go, after all."

"Huh? What's that supposed to mean?"

I was confused by how casually he'd dropped the information. Why would Nazuna be at his house? And what did he mean "he wouldn't be able to go, after all"? My mind was spinning with questions.

Yusuke leaned over, right in my face, and inexplicably began to whisper. "…She invited me to go to the fireworks display with her—or something like that."

"When?"

"Back there."

"Back where?"

"…At the pool."

I finally made the connection between the moment they'd been talking at the pool and Yusuke's constantly fluctuating mood throughout the rest of the day. Something had happened between them, it seemed.

"…So you *do* remember! But…why don't you just go with her? You like her, right?"

"Huh? What are you talking about? There's no way I'd like her. When did I ever say anything like *that*?"

"You've been saying it as long as I can remember!"

"What? Are you serious?"

"Stuff like 'I like her' and 'I wanna ask her out.' Over and over again!"

I felt myself heating up as I confronted Yusuke's feigned ignorance. My words were growing harsher and harsher.

Yusuke suddenly began pacing around in circles and shouted, "Jokes! They were all jokes! Who would ever like someone as ugly as her?! Are you stupid?! I can't believe you thought I was serious!!"

"Huh…?"

Yusuke ran off, leaving me and my frustration behind.

"I'll go ahead and tell the others!" he called back at me. "If you see Nazuna, let her know what I said, okay?!"

What was *with* him today…? Nothing he said or did made any sense! More than that, my mind was reeling with the knowledge that Nazuna had asked Yusuke out to the fireworks display. Did she like him? More than me? Even after our eyes had met *three times* in one day?

"...*Grab it.*"

Her voice flashed through my mind—the words she'd said as she lay with her eyes closed at the side of the pool.

"*Catch it.*"

I climbed up the sloped road, dragging my foot along the ground, until I arrived in front of the Azumi Clinic. The pain in my ankle had multiplied during the journey. Every step now sent shock waves through my entire right leg.

What if I really contracted tetanus? My mind was anxious as I pulled open the glass double doors of the entrance.

Just as Yusuke had forewarned, Nazuna was sitting in the waiting room.

She'd chosen a corner of a bench untouched by the harsh afternoon sun that glared in through the windows. When she heard the door open, she looked up. It was the fourth time that day for our eyes to meet.

Oh man... She's really here... Why's she wearing a yukata?

It was the first time I'd ever seen her dressed like that. The difference was stunning. The navy-blue garment was accented at the waist with a vermillion sash. It made her look very mature.

So this means she wanted to get dressed up and go see the fireworks with Yusuke...

Her eyes appeared disappointed—or perhaps even accusatory. It seemed that my arrival instead of Yusuke's had caught her by surprise.

I knew I couldn't bear that gaze very long. I sought refuge, turning to face the reception window.

"Excuse me. I'm a friend of Yusuke's..."

My throat felt dry, and the words came out like sandpaper.

"Huh? What's that?"

The chubby, middle-aged nurse was sitting on the other side of the window chewing on a cracker. Yusuke and I had both known her since we were babies, but in truth, neither of us knew her actual name. We'd always just addressed her as *Ma'am*.

"Um, I kinda injured my foot."

"Heavens! Come on in."

"Thanks…"

I sensed Nazuna's gaze at my back. It felt as if I were running away from her as I walked into the examination room.

Treating the wound took all of one minute. The nurse applied some disinfectant and a strip of gauze, then went around and around my foot with a long white bandage. My eyes took in the events, but I wasn't really paying attention.

"Tetanus? Honestly, the things that boy says… You don't need to worry about tetanus for a scrape that size…"

A putting green was rolled out along the examination room floor. Yusuke's father spoke with an air of disbelief as he sent a ball rolling toward the hole. I wasn't sure what to say, so my reply was almost involuntary.

"Oh… Ouch!"

"Come on, now, hold still." The nurse's hands had never been very gentle. Complaining that something hurt didn't make any difference. She'd just go on doing the same thing as before.

"So where's Yusuke at now?" Yusuke's father asked.

"Um, I think the fireworks display—or something like that…"

The nurse, who had finished wrapping the bandage, spoke up. "Ah, that reminds me. A girl from his class came into the waiting room."

"Fireworks display, huh? Honestly, all he thinks about is fun… We should have put him in a private school," Yusuke's father muttered as he struck another ball.

Every shot he'd taken had gone rolling off the green, and balls were now scattered all across the room. I gazed at the stray golf balls, noting how round they all were. It was an obvious thing to notice, but it struck me nonetheless. Nazuna's mysterious orb came to mind, as did the photographed fireworks from the poster.

"...Do you happen to know whether fireworks are round or flat?"

"Huh?"

I'd let the question slip out without really thinking. The nurse and Yusuke's father both stared at me.

"Um, I mean... Never mind..." I scrambled to take back what I'd said.

When I returned to the waiting room, Nazuna was sitting on the same bench, just as before. This time, she didn't look up at me. Her eyes remained fixed on the floor.

"We'll get you a bit of medicine to take at home, so just wait here," the nurse instructed from behind the window.

"Thank you."

I sat down and waited on the far edge of a bench, some distance away from Nazuna. Mixed among the calls of the dusk cicadas outside, I could also hear a distant booming—the sound of test shots courtesy of the fireworks crew.

"..."

"..."

Thirty seconds went by... Then a minute... *Come on! How long does it take to get a prescription ready?!*

I focused all my prayers on the reception window, but its little sliding door remained shut. I stole a few glances at Nazuna and saw the side of her face. She steadfastly refused to look in my direction. The *ticktock* of the waiting room's old grandfather clock was clearly audible, underscoring our awkward silence. I felt a bead of sweat roll down the back of my neck. I couldn't handle it anymore.

"...Are you waiting for Yusuke?" I called over to Nazuna.

She gave no response. I couldn't tell if she'd heard me or not. Trying my hardest to sound casual, I spilled the news. "...He's not coming."

"...I see."

Nazuna's reply came nonchalantly. Still without looking at me, she lifted herself from her seat and put a hand to a rolling suitcase waiting beside her. With a light *click-click* from her wooden sandals against the floor, she walked out of the clinic.

What was up with that huge bag? Surely she couldn't be planning on taking something so bulky to the fireworks display?

The fireworks crew seemed to have finished firing their test shots. The cries of the cicadas again dominated the waiting room.

At long last, the nurse's face appeared at the window.

"Here's your medicine. Come by again later to take care of the bill."

"Got it..."

I shoved the little paper bag containing the medicine into my pocket and walked over to the exit. When I grabbed the door handle, it felt warm, as if Nazuna's touch still lingered on it.

Outside, the oppressive heat had partially subsided. I felt the ocean air blowing up along the slope.

"I guess I should head to the shrine... Wonder if they're even still there... Or should I go directly to the lighthouse...?" I muttered to myself and began to make my way down the slope.

I was stopped short by the sight of Nazuna. I'd figured she'd be long gone, but there she was, standing in the middle of the road. Her head was pointed downward. She held one foot slightly aloft, picking at the red strap of its sandal with her toes.

"Huh?"

The word had slipped out of my mouth. Nazuna looked up.

Beyond her, the vast ocean was slowly being enveloped in faint orange. The girl floated there, between the orange sky and the faintly dyed ocean, dressed in her navy-blue *yukata*—a picture-perfect scene of evening. Her hair fluttered in the wind, and among the strands, her piercing gaze bored into me.

I stood transfixed, eyes stolen away by that single, perfect movie still. After some time, Nazuna broke the silence.

"Do you have a minute?"

"Huh?"

"Would you...walk with me for a minute?"

"Uh... Sure, I guess..."

We walked down the slope together—my mind full of questions. As we arrived at the fork where the two slopes converged, we encountered groups of people walking toward the beach and its fireworks display.

What's going on? How did it get like this...? Why am I suddenly going for a walk with Nazuna?

Was it okay for me to blow off my friends at the shrine? I wondered what they were doing right at that moment...

I found myself unable to make any conversation with Nazuna. I didn't know how to break the silence. My head felt like it was filling up with an endless stream of question marks.

On the other hand, Nazuna hadn't said a word since she invited me to walk with her, either. Maybe it was up to me to say something. I opened my mouth, but then...

"What if..."

Nazuna was walking six feet ahead of me. The little suitcase rumbled along the road behind her. She'd begun speaking in a soft voice, without turning to face me.

"Huh?"

I closed some of the distance between us in order to hear more clearly.

"What if I'd invited you instead? Would you have done the same thing as Azumi? Would you have...run away from me?"

"..."

"I decided to invite whoever swam faster in the race. The idea just came to me."

"..."

When I didn't reply, Nazuna stopped and turned around.

"I thought you'd win, Shimada."

"..."

"Why did you lose?"

Perhaps she had turned around to face me so I wouldn't be able to lie. But I had no idea what to say in the first place. All that bubbled out were a bunch of words that sounded like pitiful excuses.

"Well, I mean, you're such a fast swimmer... It caught me off guard, and..."

My answer seemed to displease Nazuna. She released her grip on the suitcase and walked two or three steps closer. I instinctively shrunk back.

"So it was my fault?"

"..."

"Was everything my fault?"

"..."

Whoa, whoa. Hang on a second. What am I supposed to say to something like that...? And what's this about how she "thought I'd win"? And when I didn't, she invited Yusuke to go with her instead? What in the world...? None of it makes any sense!

The setting sun was shining in my eyes. Nazuna was set against the light, her face mostly cast in shadow. But I thought I could faintly make out a pair of moist eyes. Was she crying...? I tried to think of something to say, but my mind was blank. No words came out.

Embarrassed, I averted my gaze. The abandoned suitcase again came into view. Now desperate for a way to steer the conversation away from what had happened at the pool, I asked about it.

"What's that thing for anyway?"

"What thing?"

Nazuna's brows furrowed unhappily. My desire to change the subject was painfully obvious, but I hurriedly pointed at the bag behind her to keep the new line of conversation moving.

"That. The suitcase."

As if only now realizing she'd left it behind, Nazuna twirled and grabbed its handle, then resumed walking in the same direction as before. I hurried after her.

"…What do you think it is?" she said over her shoulder.

The gravity of mere moments ago was gone. She spoke in a light, casual tone—but it felt forced.

"How should I know?"

"I'm running away from home."

Running away?

The news came with no buildup. She'd said it cheerfully, as if the decision was of no real consequence. It had to be a joke. I cracked a smile.

"Ah-ha-ha… Seriously?"

"Yes. I'm leaving this town."

Her pace was not hurried, but she moved with purpose. The idea occurred to me that maybe she really did intend to walk straight out of town.

I pressed, trying to feel her out. "…You're joking, right?"

"Yep. Just a joke."

"Well, which one is it?!"

"…You tell me."

Not this again…

But Nazuna's tone now was a little different from the way she'd spoken during that surreal comedy routine by the pool. If she only turned around, maybe I could tell whether she was serious or not.

She stopped walking.

Come on, turn around…

As if granting my wish, she twirled around to face me. The evening sun was now perfectly eclipsed behind her, further deepening her mask of shadow. I could still just barely make out her eyes. They were trained directly upon mine.

"Do you know why I thought you'd win?"

Welling tears transformed Nazuna's pupils into polished mirrors. I could see myself standing there in my old T-shirt with its stretched-out collar.

"…I have no idea…"

Suddenly, a new voice came from behind Nazuna, shredding through the air.

"Nazuna!!"

There was someone at the fork in the road, half running toward us.

Is that…? It looks like Nazuna's mom!

She was still too far away for me to see her expression, but the sound of her voice told me she was panicked.

Whump!

I was awoken from my daze by a dull impact. Nazuna had forced the suitcase into my arms and taken off running down the street.

"Nazuna! Get back here!!"

The loud *click-click* of the woman's sandals rushed by, quickly closing the fifty-foot gap to the clacking of her daughter's traditional footwear. She grabbed the girl by the collar.

"Nazuna! What were you thinking?!!"

Nazuna was struggling with all her might, desperate to break her mother's hold.

"Stop it! Let me *go*!! Stop it!!"

Her mother's grip held firm.

"Honestly, get ahold of yourself! Why are you always so difficult?!"

"Shut *up*! Let me go! Get your hands off me!!"

My body was frozen in place. The only time I'd ever seen two women fight before was on TV. Nazuna was hardly one to flail around like that in the first place, and though I'd only met her mother a few times before, she'd never struck me as the type prone to fits of hysteria.

Finally, Nazuna seemed to have either drained all her strength or accepted her fate. Her mother began pulling her along, hand still firmly clenched around the girl's collar. When they passed in front of me, Nazuna pleaded to me.

"Norimichi! Help me!!"

"!!"

I jolted at Nazuna's imploring use of my first name—and again at the subsequent glare I received from her mother. Every muscle in my body stiffened.

"Give me the suitcase," Nazuna's mother said, reaching for it.

The suitcase was still at my chest, bundled between my arms. My grip tightened.

"Give it to me!"

The woman's hand jumped the remaining distance to the suitcase's bandanna-wrapped handle. I twisted away from her, but I was no match for the grown woman's strength. The bag was wrested out of my arms.

The scuffle had caused the bag's clasps to pop open. As the suitcase passed from my hands to the woman's, it burst open, sending its contents flying outward.

I'd lost my balance and was also tumbling to the ground. Out of the corner of my eye, I saw a flurry of clothes, a purse, a small stuffed animal, and numerous other items disperse through the air in slow motion.

"No! I won't go! I don't want to go!!"

Nazuna's sobs filled the air as her mother dragged her away.

I had yet to recover from everything that had happened. The most I could do was to prop myself up onto my knees and watch as Nazuna and her mother receded toward the fork in the road.

Just as they left my field of vision, a familiar voice came from behind.

"Whoa! What happened?!"

I turned. Junichi and the others were running toward me. They appeared to have witnessed the whole scene and were now chattering excitedly.

"That was Nazuna, right? Holy crap! I can't believe she was screaming like that!"

"Her mom, too! What did she *do*?!"

"And what are *you* doing here, Norimichi?"

I still sat propped up on my knees, unable to speak. Rather than offering to help me up, Junichi grabbed at the collar of Minoru's shirt and, between fits of laughter, began reenacting the scene that had just unfolded.

"'Ugh, you're so difficult!'"

"'Stop it! Let me go!!'"

"Oh man. Too funny!"

Yusuke stood apart from Junichi and Minoru's improvised performance. He stared intently in the direction of the fork in the road.

I suddenly felt myself boiling over with rage. I didn't know why I was angry with Yusuke, but I lifted myself up and stormed toward him.

"Quit staring!"

I punched Yusuke in the face as hard as I could. As he

staggered backward, I rammed into him, sending him to the ground. I threw myself on top and continued to pummel his face.

I didn't know why, but for some reason, I couldn't forgive Yusuke for seeing Nazuna like that.

When I raised my right fist for the fourth punch, Junichi grabbed hold of my arm.

"Stop it!!"

"What are you doing?!!"

Kazuhiro pried me off Yusuke. I pulled and tugged against them with every ounce of strength I could muster.

"Let me go!"

Yusuke still lay on the ground with his arms covering his face, unmoving.

The two of us had fought any number of times, but until now, the fights had always had some element of playfulness. I'd never outright punched anyone in the face before.

I was filled with the adrenaline of my assault, as well as a nagging anxiety about what would come next. I didn't know what to do. I began walking away from the fork.

"Hey! Where do you think you're going?!"

I heard Junichi call out after me but ignored him.

Nazuna's belongings were strewn out before me: T-shirts, a dress, socks, camisoles, a sweater... It seemed she'd been serious about running away from home...

The stuffed animal lay streaked with dirt. Next to it, something glowed faintly.

What's that...?

It was the strange orb Nazuna had shown me. I picked it up. It seemed to grow slightly warmer, and it began to emit faint traces of light in red, green, and yellow.

"Do you know why I thought you'd win?"

Nazuna's words floated back to me.

If... Back there... If only I'd...

I lifted the orb higher and clenched my fingers around it more firmly. As if in response, the orb's light grew brighter.

If only I'd swum faster... If only I'd won against Yusuke... How would things have turned out then...?

"Hey! You gonna explain yourself?!"

"Norimichi! Say something!!"

Junichi, Minoru, and Kazuhiro were moving in on me. I faced them, drew my arm back, and shouted, "If only I'd—!!!"

Near the Fork in the Road

Norimichi lets out a shout and hurls the orb.

The orb spins as it flies down the length of the road. Rays of light stretch out from it, like beams from a lighthouse.

Whoa!!!

Junichi and the others dodge the orb. It passes between them, then slams against the noticeboard at the fork in the road, precisely where the poster of the fireworks display is hanging.

Just as the orb connects, its light grows stronger. Its colors are now strange, unearthly. The area around it begins to bend and distort into some kind of dimensional void.

Norimichi, Yusuke, Junichi, and the others are bathed in light.

NORIMICHI
?????!!!

In the distance, the propellers of the wind turbines slow to a stop…then begin to turn again, this time in the opposite direction.

There's a flash.

An egg yolk dropped on top of Norimichi's curry rises back up into its shell.

A golf ball comes rolling back toward a putter gripped by Yusuke's father.

The wheels of Norimichi's bicycle spin backward.

There's another flash, followed by images of Nazuna.

She's standing with her back turned, staring into the ocean.

She's in the classroom, looking directly into Norimichi's eyes.

She's lying down. A dragonfly is perched atop her.

                    NAZUNA
        You guys racing? I'm in.

                    NAZUNA
        Well, if *I* win, you have to do
        whatever I say.

A dragonfly rises languidly into the air.

Norimichi, Yusuke, and Nazuna dive into the pool.

"Back there… If only…I'd won…"

Wishing World 1

From the moment we dived, it was already clear who was in the lead. Nazuna crawled through the water—already six feet ahead. Even watching from behind, I could appreciate her flawless swimming form. Her arms and legs moved with a precise efficiency that widened the gap more and more.

Behind her, Yusuke and I were swimming neck and neck.

The turn's gonna be the key..., I thought, crawling forward with all my might.

Nazuna made a well-practiced turn on the far wall and headed back toward us. As Nazuna and I passed each other, I looked in her direction. She seemed not to notice and pressed onward, looking straight ahead.

Huh...?

Something felt odd... I had a nagging feeling about that moment we'd passed by each other in the water... It felt familiar—like I'd been there before. What was the name for that sort of thing...? The feeling of reliving the same moment over again...déjà... What was it again...?

While I was preoccupied with those thoughts, the far wall of the pool loomed in front of me.

I replayed Nazuna's perfect turn in my mind, blew air out through my nose, and plunged my head down toward the bottom of the pool. At the same time, I bent my knees and placed the backs of both feet squarely against the wall and pushed off as hard as I could.

Nice!

My turn was a success.

When I looked to the side, Yusuke's spin hadn't gone as planned, and he was flailing about in the water.

Limiting my breaths as much as possible, I threw everything I had into the remaining twenty-five meters.

I managed to take second place. Hurting for a good lungful of air, I brought my head up to the surface at the starting wall. A stream of water splashed in my eyes.

"Whoa! What's going on?!"

When I whipped off my goggles and looked again, Nazuna had already pulled herself out of the pool and was spraying me with water from a hose, laughing. Confronted by her carefree smile, I felt my own face turn red. I forced a glower, trying to hide my shyness.

"What are you doing?!"

"Hey, Shimada, are you going to the fireworks display tonight?"

"Huh?"

"Let's go together."

"...Why?"

"What do you mean, 'why'...?"

A hint of mischief surfaced in Nazuna's smile, and she began squirting the hose at me again.

"Come on! Quit it!"

"I'll come by your house at five. Be there."

And with that, Nazuna dropped the hose and walked away.

Huh? What did she just say?

Dumbfounded, I watched her leave. Finally, Yusuke made it to the finish line.   .

"Oh man. Right at the turn, I suddenly felt like I needed to take a dump... Huh? Where's Nazuna?"

Yusuke's words didn't even register. I stared at the abandoned hose, mentally replaying the conversation I'd just had with the girl.

Nazuna and I are going to the fireworks display together? Just the two of us? Why...?

The more I thought about what had happened, the less progress I seemed to make in comprehending it. I felt all the strength leave my body, and I sank down under the surface with air bubbles loudly burbling up from my mouth and nose. Yusuke splashed over to try to bring me back to the surface. I heard him calling in my direction, but I couldn't process what he was saying.

We'd managed to spend our entire time on cleaning duty at the pool without actually cleaning an inch. Yusuke and I made our way back to the classroom. The hallway leading to the classroom was filled with the commotion of students heading home, but the only thing I could think about was that last exchange with Nazuna.

Tonight, the two of us alone at the fireworks display... This has to be a date... Norimichi Shimada, age thirteen, in the summer of his seventh year of school, about to go on the first date of his entire life...

Yusuke, probably wondering why I was acting so weird, gave me a punch on the shoulder.

"What gives? What's up with you?"

I felt a momentary panic, remembering the suspicions he'd voiced before the race, and dodged the question. "Um... It's, uh, nothing..."

Yusuke liked Nazuna. Even if I were subjected to torture, I wouldn't dare tell him that she'd asked me out to the fireworks display.

"Look, it's Nazuna," Yusuke said.

"Huh?!"

Had he seen right through me? I was sure he had. I turned toward him, face full of surprise, only to find that he was looking in another direction entirely.

I followed his gaze to the door of the school's faculty room. In front stood Nazuna. Unlike either of us, the girl was a model student. It seemed absurd to think that Ms. Miura had asked her to stay after class. So if not because of that, then why was she there?

Yusuke cocked his head to the side, likely wondering the same thing.

"What's she doing there?"

"Could be anything…"

Nazuna appeared not to notice us staring in her direction. Her hair was still damp, and her eyes were trained intently on the door. There was a hint of nervousness in her expression—nothing like what I'd seen at the pool. Again, it felt as if I were seeing another person entirely. Her hand was closed tightly around what looked to be an envelope. Perhaps she was there to deliver it.

At long last, Nazuna raised a fist, knocked on the door, slid it open, and went inside.

In the Faculty Room

Ms. Miura sits at her desk.

>   MS. MIURA
>   (Grumpy)
>   Unbelievable…

   Mr. Mitsuishi, another teacher, sits in his
desk, directly across from hers.

>   MR. MITSUISHI
>   (In a small voice, cautious of
>   whether anyone else is nearby)
>   What's the plan today?

>   MS. MIURA
>   Huh?

>   MR. MITSUISHI
>   The fireworks display. Where are we
>   meeting each other?

>   MS. MIURA
>   (Now also cautious of their
>   surroundings)

The students were just asking me in
class whether I was going with my
boyfriend.

          MR. MITSUISHI
Seriously?

          (Grinning)
Hmmm… So I guess that means it's time
to make this public?

          MS. MIURA
Oh please. There's nothing to
announce. We were both drunk, and
that's the only reason anything…

Nazuna walks up to Ms. Miura's desk.

          NAZUNA
Excuse me, Ms. Miura?

          MS. MIURA
          (Visibly agitated)
Y-yes?! …Oh, Miss Oikawa. What do you
need?

Nazuna hands the envelope to Ms. Miura.

          MS. MIURA
What's this?

          NAZUNA
Mom… My mother told me to give it to
you.

          MS. MIURA
     (While taking the letter)
?

          NAZUNA
…

X   X   X   X

Ms. Miura is reading the letter.

                MS. MIURA
Oh, wow. They're moving away.

                MR. MITSUISHI
Who? Nazuna?

                MS. MIURA
And it's happening during summer
vacation.

                MR. MITSUISHI
Sheesh. That's pretty short notice…

                MS. MIURA
                (Still reading)
Apparently, Nazuna's mother is
getting remarried.

                MR. MITSUISHI
Really? …Man, how are you supposed to
respond to that?

                MS. MIURA
No kidding… I can't believe she made
her daughter deliver the news…

Ms. Miura's brow furrows.

As we watched Nazuna disappear into the faculty room, Yusuke punched me once more on the shoulder. It was his usual playful gesture, but this punch felt a little stronger than the last one.

"Hey."

"Huh?"

"Something happen to you?"

The question was vague, but we'd known each other so long that I immediately understood what he really wanted to ask. Yusuke had a sharp nose for stuff like that.

"Huh? What do you mean?"

I tried to keep my voice as level as possible, like I hadn't picked up on his intent. Yusuke wasn't fooled. He struck at the heart of the matter.

"Back there at the pool. You talked to Nazuna, didn't you? She didn't, like, ask you out or anything like that, right?"

"Huh?! What are you even talking about?! Why would I ever do that! Don't be stupid! And anyway, *you're* the one who likes Naz—Oikawa. There's *no way* I'd fall for a weirdo like her!"

"Whoa, what's got you all pissed off?"

He was right. What was I getting upset about?

"Um, it's nothing... Sorry."

"Yeah, whatever. Hey, are you going to the fireworks display tonight?"

"Uh, yeah. I think so."

"Wanna go together? Actually, can I just go over to your house after school?"

"Sure."

"I can't stand being at home. Lately, my dad won't shut up about studying, and it's driving me crazy. My last report card was pretty bad, and you remember how much my parents wanted to send me to private school."

"Yeah..."

"I'll come over after school—and then let's go to the fire-works display straight from there, okay?"

Giving in to Yusuke's excitement, I nodded. Only afterward did I realize the problem.

Crap... Nazuna said she'd be at my house at five. If Yusuke's there when she shows up... Wait a second, am I serious about going with Nazuna now? Whoa, whoa, whoa. There's no way that's happening. It's not like I actually said I'd go with her, right...?

I was still busy with my internal Q and A session when we made it back to the classroom. Once inside, we heard Junichi and Minoru embroiled in some kind of argument with Kazuhiro, the most diligent and passionate student in our class.

"They're flat!"

"Yeah, they're totally flat!"

"I'm telling you, they're round! Think about it! The powder inside ignites, right? And then, it explodes outward in all direc-tions. Of course they're going to be round!"

Normally, when they argued like that, I'd teasingly jump right into the fray. But I was still reeling from the encounter with Nazuna. I walked past without even acknowledging the argument and started gathering my things in preparation to go home.

"Hey, listen. If you see a firework explode from the side, does it still look round like a globe, or is it flat like a pancake?"

"What do you mean? Like a bottle rocket?" Yusuke replied to Junichi's question, disinterested.

"No! Big ones, like at a fireworks display!"

"Um...flat, I guess?"

"See?" Junichi declared proudly.

Kazuhiro, outnumbered three to one now and clearly indig-nant about Yusuke's lackadaisical response, was about to boil over.

"Don't be ridiculous! They're totally round! Norimichi, what do you think?"

His question confronted me so unexpectedly, I struggled to

respond. I'd gathered the gist of the conversation: Would fireworks shot up into the sky at a professional show always look round, no matter where you were standing, or was that shape dependent on the angle you were watching from? That's what they seemed to be arguing…but who even cared?!

I couldn't just say that outright, so I gave a half-hearted response instead.

"Huh? I dunno."

"Well *think* about it!" Junichi pressed.

"Sorry…"

Even as I apologized to Junichi, I was still thinking about Nazuna. She was coming over at five… But Yusuke was coming over to hang out, too… What was I supposed to do? I shot a glance at Yusuke. Our eyes met: He'd been staring at me. I felt uncomfortable under his searching gaze, so I pretended to concentrate on packing my things into my school bag.

Kazuhiro and the others continued their argument, no longer paying attention to us. It registered as background noise to me.

"All right, so have any of you ever seen a flat firework before?!"

"I have!" Minoru announced.

"Oh, like *you'd* know anything, Minoru."

"It's true. Last year, I watched the fireworks display from my grandpa's yard. The fireworks were totally flat. Grandpa said it was because his house is at a bad angle for viewing the show."

"See? If his grandpa says so, it has to be true!"

The fireworks argument continued to stream by me, somehow managing to become even less interesting. I was trying to come up with a plan for the Nazuna situation when Nazuna herself walked in through the classroom's back door. She seemed to have finished up whatever business she had at the faculty room. She walked to her desk, her hair still slightly damp.

"!!"

Thump!

It felt as if my heart had caused my entire body to jolt. Nazuna had turned straight toward my desk and was staring at me. My immediate reaction was to focus on something else: the schoolyard outside the windows. I'd spent the entire term sneaking glances at her, trying to be careful she didn't notice. It seemed my bad habit of glancing away had stuck.

Now afraid that my evasion had been too obvious, I tried to casually turn back. She'd already finished packing and was on her way out of the classroom.

As I watched her walk away, she didn't bother to turn around again. A strange mixture of relief and guilt flooded through me.

"Then it's decided!! We all meet at Moshimo Shrine at five PM! Norimichi, you're coming, too, right?"

The others seemed to have reached some kind of agreement. Junichi's excited voice called out to me, pulling me back to reality.

"Huh? What's going on?"

"Weren't you listening?! We're going to Moshimo Lighthouse! We're gonna see for ourselves whether fireworks are round or flat!"

"We are?"

"Yeah, we are! And if they're flat, Kazuhiro's gonna do all our summer homework."

"Whoo-hoo!!" Minoru raised his hands up above his short frame, giving Junichi and Yusuke high fives as he cheered.

Kazuhiro muttered something about how someone "better be serious about taking that up-skirt pic of Ms. Miura." I didn't really care whether fireworks were round or flat—and what in the world did that have to do with an up-skirt pic anyway?

I knew I could ask Yusuke to fill me in on the details, but I didn't want him to know I hadn't been listening to the conversation. I looked out the window again to try to keep them from asking me any more questions about whatever they were discussing.

The baseball club was practicing in the schoolyard, and that was when I saw her. Walking right through the center of the practice was Nazuna.

She always carried herself with good posture, but in that moment, it seemed like her back was held even a little straighter than usual... Maybe it was just my imagination.

The five of us split up at the unbelievably huge, age-old beech tree that marked the fork in the road.

"Five o'clock! Don't be late! Minoru and I will start heading over early, around four."

"Yeah, we got it!"

Junichi and Minoru sped away to the left, and Kazuhiro to the right.

"All right, so we'll hang out at your place until then. You've got some cola or something to drink, right?"

Yusuke hoisted himself up onto the seat of his mountain bike.

"We might not have anything but tea."

"Oh man. The tea at your house is always so blah."

"Shut up," I answered, half laughing.

When I lifted my right foot up to its pedal, a strange sensation came over me.

Huh? Didn't something happen to my ankle...?

I reached down and felt my right ankle, but nothing seemed to be wrong. I couldn't figure out why the thought had occurred to me. When I straightened back up, the town noticeboard flashed in the corner of my eye. A poster was stuck to it, advertising that night's fireworks display. For some reason, the poster seemed strange, too.

It wasn't like I'd ever stopped to look at it carefully, but the photos of multicolored firework explosions spreading across the sky seemed flatter than they should have been...

"Norimichi? What's up?"

I'd fallen silent as I stared intently at the poster. Concerned, Yusuke peered into my face.

"Hey, did the fireworks poster always look this way?"

"What do you mean?"

I didn't exactly understand what about the poster felt strange, and I didn't think I'd be able to explain it to Yusuke, so I dodged the question.

"Um...never mind."

"Whatever. I'm gonna get changed, then I'll be over."

"Okay."

Yusuke and I pedaled away in our separate directions. The strange feeling in my ankle was gone when I pushed down on the pedal again. Satisfied that it must have been my imagination, I began pedaling harder. Suddenly, the date with Nazuna returned to mind.

Crap... What was I going to do about her?

At Nazuna's Home
(Public Housing)

Nazuna walks into the living room.

>   NAZUNA
>   Anyone home?

A middle-aged man sitting on the sofa turns
toward her.

>   MAN
>   Welcome back.

>   NAZUNA
>   …!

Nazuna's mother emerges from the kitchen,
where she has been preparing tea.

>   NAZUNA'S MOTHER
>   Where are your manners? Say hello.

>   MAN
>   Oh, did you have school today?
>   Must've been pretty hot. I brought
>   some cake over. Shall we all have a
>   piece?

The man is Nazuna's mother's new fiancé. He picks up a box of assorted cake slices and moves toward Nazuna.

                    MAN
        Do you see one you like, sweetie?
            (He smirks a little as he
                addresses her.)

                  NAZUNA
        ...

Nazuna heads toward her room without responding.

              NAZUNA'S MOTHER
        Nazuna!

The girl's door slams shut.

              NAZUNA'S MOTHER
        ...I'm sorry about that.

                    MAN
        Oh, don't worry. It's all right.

        ✕   ✕   ✕   ✕

Nazuna's room is dimly lit from behind the drawn curtains.

                  NAZUNA
        ...

The conversation between her mother and the man is still faintly audible.

               MAN'S VOICE
        Did you already make the arrangements
        at her school?

        NAZUNA'S MOTHER'S VOICE
Yes. I let her homeroom teacher know
today.

        MAN'S VOICE
It must be hard for her, leaving all
her friends behind.

        NAZUNA'S MOTHER'S VOICE
Goodness, no. That girl hardly has
any friends. Nothing to worry about.

        MAN'S VOICE
What about a boyfriend?

        NAZUNA'S MOTHER'S VOICE
                (Laughing)
At her age?!

        MAN'S VOICE
I wouldn't be so sure. You never know
about girls these days.

                NAZUNA
                (Disgusted)
    ...

Nazuna stands and opens her dresser. She
pulls her *yukata* out from the back.

She strips off her uniform and begins to
put on the *yukata*.

A makeshift sign reading CLOSED FOR TODAY dangled from the storefront door. I circled around behind the shop and pulled our spare house key out from the mailbox. When I opened the door, I was met with the muggy air of a house left unoccupied during a summer day.

"Why does it have to be so hot?"

I threw my sweat-soaked button-down shirt into the laundry basket, then walked into the kitchen. I opened the fridge, expecting to see my half-finished bottle of cola from the day before. It was right where I'd left it. I reached out for it, then stopped, thinking I ought to leave it for Yusuke.

Next, I pulled open the freezer and saw a box of my dad's favorite ice pops: Watermelon Bars. There was only one left in the box, and I decided to take it.

Whoever came up with the idea of an ice pop that looks just like a wedge of cut watermelon, with an easy-to-eat triangular shape and little chocolate "seeds" inside, was a genius... Except... Huh?

When I pulled the bar out from its plastic wrapper, it wasn't the normal wedge shape I was used to. It was *cylindrical*—like a normal ice pop. Had the freezer cut out for a while, causing the bar to melt and then refreeze?

The cylinder seemed too perfect for that. The ice pop had to have been made that way. Maybe it was shaped like that for some limited-edition campaign to drum up sales, or maybe they made small batches of special shapes sometimes and mixed them in with the normal ones, and it was like finding a rare holographic trading card in a booster pack.

Still shirtless, and now biting into my super-rare Watermelon Bar, I climbed the stairs to my room. It was even hotter on the second floor. I slid open the window in my room, but the warm summer air that blew in didn't do much to help.

Holding the Watermelon Bar between my teeth, I pulled

down my elementary school graduation album from the bookshelf. I pulled the album out of its sleeve and opened it, landing by coincidence on the particular section I was looking for.

It was a page I'd looked at over and over again, filled with pictures from our school trip to Nikko. Our class had been split into groups for the field trip, and Nazuna and I had been assigned together. Our little group had gathered for a photo in front of the Toshogu Shrine. I'd just happened to be standing next to Nazuna when it was taken—well, no, that wasn't right. I'd pretended it was by happenstance, but really I'd made sure I was next to her... In the photo, Nazuna stood expressionless, while I had a wide-open grin and was flashing a peace sign.

Nazuna and I had first met two years ago, over our fifth grade summer vacation.

Nazuna's father was born and raised in Moshimo. He'd left to go work in Tokyo, but he eventually quit his job there and returned to open a surf shop along the coast of our little town. My own dad used to be a surfer, too, long before he took the reins of our family's worn-down fishing shop. Back in high school, he'd been friends with Nazuna's dad.

Shortly after Nazuna's family moved to Moshimo, the three of them paid a visit to my dad's shop to say hello. Nazuna had stood shyly hiding behind her parents.

In fact, I remembered I'd been eating a Watermelon Bar that day, too. I'd sunk my teeth into it as I looked at the girl from behind the doorway.

Her mother had said, "This is our daughter, Nazuna. Go on and introduce yourself, honey."

And Nazuna had politely bowed and said hello. In contrast, I'd stayed in the living room, furtively peering out at our visitors. If my mom and dad had asked me to introduce myself like Nazuna's parents had, I wouldn't have known what to say. It wasn't like we were automatically friends just because our parents were.

Nazuna had been wearing a white summer dress and a straw hat that day. Her dark hair had shone, and her milky skin had seemed almost translucent... Not to sound cliché, but it was the first time I'd seen a perfect-looking girl, like someone who could have come straight out of a TV show or a commercial.

Then, as I'd sat in the living room, staring at that perfect girl with a vacant look on my face, my dad had said the most embarrassing thing ever.

"Hey, Norimichi! You and Nazuna are in the same grade. You must be pretty excited to be going to school with a cutie like this."

Tipped off by my dad's comment, Nazuna had looked toward the living room, finally realizing I was there. Our eyes had met.

Mortified by my dad's comment, I'd announced, "I don't know what you're talking about!" and escaped into another room.

That's right... That was the first time our eyes met...

I was reaching one finger out to touch a photo of Nazuna when I heard the drumming of feet on the stairway.

"Norimichi!"

I scrambled to close the album and tossed it down onto the floor. At that exact moment, the door slid open, and Yusuke burst in.

"Yo!"

"What do you mean, 'Yo'?! What do you think you're doing?!"

"You guys gotta take better precautions. The back door was unlocked."

"That doesn't mean you can just waltz right in, you know."

"What were you doing anyway? Why are you standing around in your room half-naked?"

"...No reason."

"Oh man, a Watermelon Bar. Gimme."

Yusuke pulled the ice pop out of my hands, then sat down and turned on the Wii. Using my foot, I surreptitiously slid the graduation album underneath my bed so Yusuke wouldn't notice it. Then, I sat down next to him. I looked at the Watermelon Bar he'd taken and was reminded of my earlier confusion.

"Hey, isn't that bar shaped kinda weird?"

"How so?"

"It's probably a rare special edition. Like one in ten thousand or something."

"What's so rare about it?"

"It's round. Not shaped like a triangle."

"Huh? Watermelon Bars are always round."

Was he being serious?

I mean, I knew his grades last term had been pretty bad, but his comment made me start to worry whether his brain was working right. Yusuke, for his part, was staring back at me with the same look of incredulity. His eyes seemed to say, *Is this guy serious?* He fished his hand in the garbage can and pulled out the wrapper I'd just thrown away.

"What are you talking about? They've always been wedge shaped. That's how it is on the wrapper!"

...*Huh?* The wrapper design, which I'd seen a million times since I was little, was supposed to have a wedge-shaped bar on it—one that looked just like a real piece of watermelon. But when I looked at the wrapper Yusuke held up...the bar was cylindrical.

"They've always been round, ever since we were kids. Are you feeling okay?"

"..."

Is this what it feels like to step into the twilight zone?

"Anyway, we're supposed to be at the shrine at five. So if we leave here ten to five, that should be enough, right?"

"Uh, yeah."

I was reminded I didn't have time to worry about the Watermelon Bar. The real problem was Nazuna. She'd be showing up soon... What time was it now?

I looked at the alarm clock on my desk. It had just turned 4:10.

At Moshimo Shrine

Moshimo Shrine lies just beyond a train crossing for the Moshimo Railway line.

An old single-car train slowly rumbles by with a leisurely *click-clack* coming from its wheels.

Street vendors are busy setting up their stalls for the festival.

Among them, one stall is already open for business: an *oden* soup vendor.

A coarse but friendly man sits at the stall, drinking a glass of hard liquor and speaking with Junichi and Minoru.

> JUNICHI
> Seriously?!

> MAN
> Yeah, completely flat.

> MINORU
> We were right!

Kazuhiro arrives at the stall.

                    KAZUHIRO
          Hey. Were you waiting long?

                    JUNICHI
          Hey… Huh? What's up with you?

                    MINORU
          Why're you dressed like that?

                    KAZUHIRO
Huh?

     Kazuhiro is wearing an almost comically large
hiking backpack. On his head is a helmet, and in
his hands are an ice ax and a large flashlight.

                    KAZUHIRO
          What do you mean? We're going on,
          like, an adventure, right?

     Junichi and Minoru clutch their sides with
laughter.

                    KAZUHIRO
          Come on! Quit laughing!

                    JUNICHI
          Oh yeah, and guess what we just
          heard? This guy says fireworks are
          flat!

                    KAZUHIRO
          What?

                    MINORU
          Yeah. This gentleman is, not to put
          too fine a point on it, a genuine,
          professional pyrotechnician!

The man drinking liquor is wearing a jacket emblazoned with the name of a fireworks company.

                    JUNICHI
          And a genuine pyrotechnician's word
          is as good as gold!

                    MAN
          Hiccups loudly.

Over the next forty minutes, Yusuke's Bowser consistently won every *Mario Kart* race. That wasn't usually the case. In pretty much every game we played, our scores were about even. But that day, the game was the furthest thing from my mind. Nazuna would arrive soon... What was I going to do?

"Oh, look. It's almost five."

Yusuke seemed to realize how much time had passed, too. He checked the clock while taking another swig from his plastic bottle of cola. It was still light outside, but the calls of the morning cicadas had petered out in favor of the dusk cicadas'.

"Yeah, looks like it."

I answered with a carefree tone, but the fact that so much time had passed and I *still* didn't have a plan weighed heavy on my mind.

How am I gonna deal with Yusuke? Wait... So does this mean I'm planning to actually go to the fireworks display with Nazuna?

Just then, Yusuke piped up. "Hey, wanna skip going to the shrine altogether?" He slapped at a mosquito on his arm.

"Huh?" I responded. I was confused for a moment, but then I remembered that was how Yusuke always acted. It was pretty common for him to change plans at the drop of a hat, depending on how he was feeling.

He went on without a trace of concern about the promise he'd made to our friends. "You know, does it really even matter whether fireworks are round or flat? Let's just go to the beach and enjoy the show."

"Uh, yeah..."

"Seriously, though. Of course fireworks are *flat*." Yusuke suddenly made the declaration as if it was the most obvious thing in the world.

I couldn't help my surprise. "Huh? Really?"

"Yeah! Whoa, whoa, you don't really think...?"

"No! I mean, I dunno...," I faltered.

Yusuke reached out and grabbed a fan that was sitting on my bed. There was a photo of a perfectly round firework printed on its surface.

"Think about it. They explode out in a circle, right? But if you look at it from the side, like this, of course it's gonna look flat!"

Yusuke held the image of the firework in front of my face, then rotated the fan ninety degrees to the side. As to be expected, the firework on the fan looked flat when it was turned sideways.

"Right?!"

"Yeah, I guess…"

That last, confident proclamation from Yusuke almost had me convinced. Except…

Kazuhiro had pointed out that the powder inside the firework exploded and… How did he describe it? Like radiation? No, that wasn't quite right… Anyway, didn't the explosion spread outward in a big, round pattern?

"See? So there's no reason to go all the way out to the lighthouse. Let's just forget about it. And hey, close the window. This place is swarming with mosquitoes."

"Okay."

As I stood, I mulled over this new turn of events.

Wait… If we aren't going to the shrine anymore, then there's no reason for Yusuke to be here.

If I made him leave my house now, then I wouldn't have to worry when Nazuna showed up in a few minutes… As for the date with her, that could wait. I'd figure that part out after she arrived.

"You know what? You're right. And hey, I just remembered I've got some stuff I need to take care of today any—"

When I put my hand on the window, I saw the figure of a girl wearing a *yukata* in the distance. She was pulling a suitcase along behind her… Nazuna! *Oh man! She's here already!*

My mind racing, I slid the window shut… What was I going

to do? She wasn't far. It wouldn't take more than a minute, maybe even forty-five seconds, before she was in front of the house...

Think! Think, dang it!

"Huh? 'Stuff to take care of'? What do *you* have going on?"

Yusuke downed the last of the cola.

"Um... Yeah! I was just thinking, I'm gonna go buy some drinks. We're gonna play some more *Mario Kart*, right?"

"Nah, I don't need anything else. I'm not thirsty anymore."

"No, no, no. I mean, that one was already flat, wasn't it? I felt kinda bad giving it to you. I'm gonna go buy a fresh one, so wait here."

"Really? Thanks."

"Don't mention it."

Even I felt like my argument hadn't made any sense, but Yusuke had agreed, and now was my chance. I grabbed some change out of one of my drawers and stuffed it into the pocket of my shorts.

When I tried to leave the room, Yusuke spoke up again. "Whoa, you're going out dressed like that?"

"Huh?"

I followed his finger and took a good look at myself. He was right. I still hadn't put on a shirt since I'd arrived home.

"Um..."

"Are you feeling okay?"

"Ah-ha-ha-ha..." I gave him a sheepish grin as I reached toward my bed and snatched the Uniqlo T-shirt I used as a pajama top. I awkwardly hustled down the stairs in a flurry of loud thumps.

Nazuna would probably go to the storefront first. She'd see the sign saying it was closed and then circle around back... And that meant she was probably nearing the door just then!

Praying that I'd made it in time, I threw open the back door. I saw a right hand reaching out toward the doorbell and instinctively grabbed it by the wrist.

"!!"

Nazuna's eyes were wide with surprise. She looked from my face then down to where my hand gripped her wrist. She opened her mouth to speak, but I held a finger to my lips.

"Shhhh..." I continued to hold her as the tiny, hoarse warning escaped my lungs.

Apparently growing more and more uncertain of the situation, Nazuna tilted her head to the side. Her braids swayed back and forth like pendulums.

It was the first time I'd ever seen her in a *yukata* and the first time I'd ever touched her. I was shocked by how thin her wrist felt in my hand. But the important thing at that moment was to make sure Yusuke stayed unaware of the situation.

"Yusuke's here."

"Huh?"

"Let's go outside."

I released my grasp and turned to close the door. I stepped out onto the path in front of my house. Nazuna followed wordlessly. The calls of the morning cicadas were gone; only the dusk cicadas were singing now.

"Sorry, he just suddenly came over and wanted to hang out..."

"...Well, what are you going to do? Are you canceling on me?" Her response was a bit prickly. Yeah, my explanation did sound like an excuse.

I took a step forward to escape her piercing gaze.

"J-just hang on a sec. I'm thinking..."

In truth, I had no idea what to do. What would happen if I just left with her? What would Yusuke do if I didn't come back?

A window rumbled open above us.

"Hey, Norimichi!"

"!!"

I looked up and saw Yusuke sticking his head out the window. Nazuna seemed to be hidden by the eaves. He hadn't noticed her.

"I was thinking, we oughtta go to the shrine, after all."

"Huh?"

"I mean, they're all expecting us."

"…You gotta be kidding…"

"I'll come down. Let's head over." Yusuke closed the window as he made his latest announcement.

What on earth? Why's he suddenly…?

I stared at the window in disbelief. A small tug came at the hem of my T-shirt. Nazuna had pressed her back up against the wall during my conversation with Yusuke. She was peering into my face now.

"…What are we going to do?"

Her eyes were not burning with anger. Rather, they seemed to be clouded with sadness.

What was I going to do?

Wait… Why is it up to me to decide anyway?

The whole situation felt absurd. *I* didn't ask to go to the fireworks display with Nazuna—or even to go to Moshimo Lighthouse with Yusuke and the others. *They all pressed that stuff onto me! Why did Nazuna even ask me to go see the fireworks in the first place…? It was just because I came in second place at the pool, right…? So if… If it hadn't been me, and Yusuke had been in second place instead, then she'd have invited…*

The door clicked open, and I heard Yusuke shoving his feet into his sneakers.

She'd have invited him *instead?*

My mind went blank at the thought. I impulsively grabbed Nazuna's hand and began to run.

"This way!"

"Huh?!"

Between my tugging and the weight of her luggage, Nazuna almost lost her balance. I yanked her along to the front of the store. I hastily righted my bicycle, which had been leaning against the door.

"Get on!"

"Huh?"

"Just do it!"

"But…"

While Nazuna was hesitating, Yusuke's voice rang out from the back of the house.

"Where'd you go…? Hey! Norimichi!"

I snatched the suitcase from Nazuna's hands and balanced it across the bike's front basket.

I turned to Nazuna once more—this time looking her directly in the eyes.

"Get on."

I saw her indecision melt away as soon as our eyes met. The clouds of sadness from before were nowhere to be found. A burst of confidence spread across her face, and she nodded.

"Got it."

She circled an arm around my waist and hoisted herself up on the narrow luggage rack behind the saddle, her legs dangling to one side.

I pushed into the pedals. I wasn't used to the extra weight of a second passenger, and the handlebars wavered unsteadily. As soon as the wheels hit the grade of the slope, however, the ride evened out, and we began to pick up speed.

I heard Yusuke's footsteps rushing around to the front of the store.

"Hey! …Huh? …*Nazuna?* …Norimichi! What the heck are you—?"

Yusuke's voice was drowned out by the roar of the wind whipping by.

As the slope became more intense, so did our speed. Nazuna's hand tightened on my waist, and I felt her draw her body closer to my back. I'd never had a girl ride on the back of my bike before. The fact that it was *Nazuna* dawned on me anew. I felt her warmth spread from my back and around to my stomach. The handlebars wobbled again as my concentration shifted, and Nazuna let out a small yelp. With a jolt, I refocused my attention on steering.

As we continued downward, the sea drew nearer. I could smell the ocean air; it mingled with the scent of Nazuna's hair fluttering behind me.

Nazuna called forward in a loud voice, "Hey!"

"Yeah?"

"Where are we going?!"

I hadn't thought about a destination until she posed the question. I'd been driven by instinct back at the house.

"...No idea."

"What kind of answer is that?"

"I don't know!"

I caught the faint sound of her laughing softly behind me. Apparently, it was contagious; I found myself laughing, too.

We heard a distant *boom...pop...boom...pop* mixed in with the wind. I realized it must have been the sound of test shots courtesy of the fireworks crew.

The echoes returned from the mountainside, and I turned my head in that direction only to see the slowly turning propellers of the wind turbines. For the first time since they'd been erected two years ago, I felt a strange sensation looking at them.

"Hey."

"What?"

"The wind farm... Did the propellers always turn like that?"

"Huh? I don't know."

"Aren't they supposed to go clockwise?"

"I just told you. I have no idea."

"Oh..."

Neither of us seemed to know anything about anything. I didn't know why I was doing this, and I didn't know what to do going forward. But all of that somehow felt like minor details. It was all stuff that didn't really matter right now.

What I was certain of was that I was on a bicycle with Nazuna, riding along the coast.

If only this could last forever...

The thought felt like something out of a cheap pop song, but it was soon pushed aside by Nazuna's voice from behind.

"Hey... Head toward the station!"

At the Shrine

A train rolls by.

The crossing bars rise up, and Yusuke walks over the tracks, heading toward Junichi, Minoru, and Kazuhiro, who are sitting on the stairs leading up to the shrine building.

> JUNICHI
> Man, why are you so late?!

> YUSUKE
> Shut up!!

> JUNICHI
> Huh? Why are you all pissed off?

> YUSUKE
> I'm not pissed off, so just shut up!!!!

> MINORU
> Hey, where's Norimichi?

                    YUSUKE
...Hell if I know!!

                    JUNICHI
Huh? Seriously, what's got you all
steamed?

The Moshimo Railway line was a single track running along the coast from the city to our small town. Moshimo Station was the last stop.

In the past, it had carried droves of tourists headed for swims at the beach or visits to the town's iconic lighthouse, but since then, it had become run-down and lonely, hardly used by anyone other than local residents. There had been talk of shutting the line down within a few years. The story gained some credence when Moshimo Station had been converted to a self-pay, completely unstaffed stop two years ago. .

When Nazuna and I arrived, we sat on the bench in the old wooden waiting room, doing nothing in particular. Our only companions were the station's lonely machines, selling tickets and drinks. I glanced around the room, desperate to find some con-versation piece I could use to break the awkward silence between us. My eyes fell on a poster advertising the day's fireworks display.

That's right… I completely forgot!

I wondered if Junichi and the others were already on their way to the lighthouse.

The hands of the clock had just passed five. I flitted my eyes from the clock to Nazuna. She was sitting just far enough away on the bench that another person could have fit between us.

Even though she was the one who asked to go to the station, she hadn't made any motion to buy a ticket once we'd arrived. I had no idea what she intended to do there. Wasn't our plan to go see the fireworks?

"…So by the way…"

"Huh?"

"Are we still planning to go see the fireworks display?"

"…Do you want to?"

"What do you mean? *You* were the one who said you wanted to go."

"Did I say that?"

Nazuna giggled. I couldn't tell whether she was faking it or if she'd really forgotten. Her *yukata* was slightly disheveled, probably from all the running and riding on my bicycle. The modest, grown-up design of her *yukata* seemed to suit her well, but I knew I'd never be able to summon up the courage to tell her that. I found I wasn't even able to keep looking at her. My eyes wandered back down to my feet.

Beyond Nazuna's sandals lay the little suitcase with its checkered pattern. It struck me that a *yukata* and a suitcase were an odd combination.

"That, um…"

"Huh?"

"That suitcase. What's it for?"

"Oh, this?"

Nazuna pulled the suitcase closer to her and unlatched its metal clasps. The contents stuffed inside burst outward and littered the floor.

"Whoa!"

I was surprised to see T-shirts, a dress, socks, camisoles, a sweater…a stuffed animal, and a little pouch, like a…cosmetics bag? Was that the right word?

At any rate, none of it seemed like stuff you'd take to a fireworks display. What on earth was she planning?

"Ah, shoot. It fell open."

Nazuna crouched on the ground and began to gather the things strewn about. When she picked up the stuffed animal, she turned to me with a mischievous grin.

"Aren't you going to help?"

"Uh… Okay."

I squatted down and, as instructed, started picking up shirts, socks, and assorted items nearest me.

I'd never touched women's clothes, except for maybe my mom's. Nazuna's filled my nostrils with a faint, sweet smell—far unlike the plain detergent used to wash my own clothes. I'd caught traces of that fragrance when we were on the bicycle. It was Nazuna's scent.

Nazuna stood once the bag had been repacked. She began examining the timetable posted on one wall. "So where to, then?"

She had murmured quietly. Her words seemed half directed toward me and half meant for no one in particular. But we were the only two people in the station, so I decided she must be talking to me.

"Um, are you planning to catch a train?"

"Isn't that the point of coming to a station?"

"But I mean, the fireworks display—"

...was what you invited me to, I started to say, but Nazuna cut me off with an excited proposal.

"How about Tokyo? Or Osaka?"

"Huh?"

"Anywhere's fine with me. But the farther away, the better."

Tokyo? Osaka?

I had trouble processing the words themselves, since they were so far removed from what I was expecting to hear. I was starting to panic. Nazuna was smiling with what appeared to be her usual cheerful smile. However, something about it felt hollow to me. We were sitting right next to each other, but I was having trouble grasping how she truly felt.

I concentrated as hard as I could, both to keep from losing myself to frustration, and to try to work out the situation logically.

Maybe she'd never planned on going to the fireworks display in the first place. *But what is this talk about Tokyo or Osaka...? Is she planning to...? No way...*

"Are you running away?"

A part of me felt like I'd finally put two and two together: the contents of her suitcase and the places she was talking about.

"That's it, isn't it? You're running away from home, aren't you?"

My words were growing more and more confident, until Nazuna brushed them all aside.

"No, I'm not."

"Then what *are* you doing?"

Nazuna was frowning, clearly serious. My own voice was getting more agitated with each question I asked. We were at a train station that only headed out of town—toward the city. Her bag was full of clothes, and she was talking about Tokyo or Osaka... If this wasn't running away, then what was it? After a bit of silence, Nazuna mumbled a single word.

"...Eloping."

Eloping...? My brain was reeling from yet another unexpected word. I was having trouble parsing what it even meant.

"...Eloping? Is that when two lovers...die together?"

"No! That's a suicide pact!"

On a Country Road

The sun is sinking behind the mountains. Along the ridge, ten or so wind turbines stand, their propellers slowly revolving.

Yusuke and company are dragging their feet along the path.

The lighthouse feels much farther than anticipated, and the whole group's mood has soured.

Yusuke is twirling a tree branch he picked up along the way.

> KAZUHIRO
> (Speaking of his backpack)
> This is way too heavy… Hey, guys, let's take a little break…

> JUNICHI
> Oh, come on! You were the one who said we should come out here.

> KAZUHIRO
> (Now taking off his pack)
> I don't think I can go on…

MINORU
What's in there anyway?

Minoru walks closer and opens the backpack.

Inside is a tightly packed assortment of bananas, apples, snack foods, bottled drinks, and so on.

JUNICHI
(Also peering inside)
What's all this for?

MINORU
You planning to set up shop or something?

Sounds of test shots come from the direction of the fireworks display.

YUSUKE
Hey! Get off your butts, or we'll miss it!!

The other three boys recoil a bit at Yusuke's harsh tone.

JUNICHI
Why is he so riled up?

The restrooms on the train platform were set off by a series of thin, wooden walls. Nazuna's voice sounded through one of them.

"Girls can find work no matter where they are, you know."

I stood with my back to the wall, as if on guard duty. But my brain was focused entirely on the other side of that wall. Nazuna's voice, her breaths, and the rustle of her changing all resonated clearly on the otherwise empty platform. I heard the shuffling of fabric. One end of her *obi* sash was flung over the wall and dangled there.

"All I have to do is lie about my age and say I'm eighteen."

"You don't look eighteen."

"You don't think so?"

Next, the *yukata* flopped over the side.

Does this mean...she's in her underwear right now?

For a moment, my mind attempted to paint the picture. I stopped in panic, fearing my silence would betray my thoughts, and searched for something to say.

"But, uh...where would you find work anyway?"

"Probably in the nightlife, I guess... At a hostess club? Or a bar?"

"I don't think it's that easy..."

I was having trouble containing myself. I glanced down at the gap between the wooden wall and the platform floor. I could see Nazuna's bare feet trading her wooden sandals for a pair of bright-red leather...pumps? Is that what they're called? Even the clumsy, obviously callow way she moved her feet struck me as alluring, and I found myself struggling even more to concentrate on the conversation.

I estimated we couldn't be more than a foot and a half apart at that moment, despite the wall that separated us. A foot and a half away, Nazuna was taking off her *yukata*... I couldn't stand it any longer and walked across the platform toward the tracks.

I heard the *click-clack* of the train approaching from afar. I raised my voice to make sure Nazuna could hear me beyond the wall.

"Hey, the train's coming!"

"I know. I just finished…"

I turned to find Nazuna slowly emerging from behind the wall.

She was in a black cocktail dress. The neck dipped down far enough to reveal a slight amount of cleavage. On her feet were the red pumps I'd caught a glimpse of earlier. She'd undone her braids, and now her wavy hair hung around her shoulders, rustling softly in the wind.

She hadn't only changed her outfit. Her lips were red, evidence of the makeup she must have applied in the little restroom. She was a completely different person from the Nazuna I'd walked into the station with moments earlier.

Nazuna seemed to know it, too. Her face carried a trace of embarrassment. She mumbled a question without looking in my direction.

"So? Do I look eighteen?"

I had no idea whether she could pass for eighteen or not, but in that moment, on the platform of the station enveloped in fading daylight, with her dress and her hair fluttering in a slight breeze, she was…beautiful.

I felt like I'd finally grasped the true meaning of the word. *Beautiful.*

"I do, right? I look like I'm eighteen?"

"Uh…well…um…"

I racked my brain but wasn't coming up with any real words. Even if I'd been able to, I was scared I'd say something inane if I opened my mouth. I simply stood there, trying to burn that image of Nazuna into my mind.

Nazuna, still looking away, pulled something out of her pocket.

"Look at this."

"Huh?"

Nazuna held out the mysterious orb from before. It seemed to appear a bit different than it had in the afternoon, but it might have been due to the dimness of approaching night.

"...Yeah, you showed me earlier at the pool..."

"I found it in the ocean this morning."

The scene I'd witnessed from my bicycle that morning floated to mind: Nazuna, standing at the water's edge.

"For some reason...when I found this, my mind was set. I decided to leave."

"..."

"No, wait... That's not quite right... It was when you won the race, Shimada. That's when I decided to leave."

"Huh?"

Too many things had happened to me in the span of one day. The events of just hours ago felt like distant memories. That morning I'd seen Nazuna, and later in the classroom, in the middle of my friends' silly argument, our eyes had met. She'd shown me the orb at the side of the pool. Then, I'd smashed my foot during the race, causing me to lose to Yusuke...

No, wait. I won the race. But... Huh? What's this weird feeling?

I'd felt like this earlier in the day, too. After school, when Yusuke and I were going home, there had been a momentary pain in my right ankle, even though I was sure I hadn't injured it. It was the same odd sensation.

But I was *sure* I won against Yusuke. Then, Nazuna had asked me to go to the fireworks display with her...

And what happened after that...?

We'd returned to the classroom, and Junichi, Kazuhiro, and Minoru were talking about whether fireworks were round or flat... When I'd gone home, Yusuke was already there, waiting for me... After that, I went to the clinic, and they took a look at my...

No. I didn't get hurt, so why would I go to the clinic...?

We'd been at my house, and Nazuna had shown up... Then, at the fork in the road, Nazuna's mother came and took her away...

Huh? Then why is Nazuna here with me right now?

Whoo-whoo! The lonely, one-car Moshimo Railway train blew its whistle and drew near.

"Come with me."

Nazuna looked me right in the eyes.

I looked back. I knew those pleading eyes.

"..."

I wasn't able to reply, though. My thoughts were still all tangled up.

I seemed to be holding a mix of two days' worth of memories. It was as if I'd lived two separate lives, one down the right fork of a road and the other down the left.

Where had it started? Where had things diverged into right and left?

The *click-clack* of the train was now accompanied by the screech of its brakes. The train slid slowly into position alongside the platform.

Soon it would be completely stopped, and the doors would open.

When that happened, what was I going to do?

Would I get on with Nazuna?

If I did, where would we go?

Nazuna stared intently at me, waiting for a response that hadn't yet come to me. I thought I sensed tears welling up. I felt like someone had taken an egg beater to the insides of my head, but I desperately wanted to answer her. I opened my mouth to speak.

Just then, a shrill voice emanated from the direction of the ticket gate, ripping apart our shared moment.

"Nazuna!!"

That voice... It's so familiar...

I turned to find Nazuna's mother, and behind her was a middle-aged man I'd never seen before.

They ran past the unmanned ticket gate and headed toward us. The anger on the woman's face was as plain as day. That expression...the sight of her running toward me...my body stiffening... They were all familiar.

Whump!

I'd been standing dazed, overwhelmed by the bizarre impression that I was reliving the same moment over again, until a dull impact woke me. Nazuna's suitcase had slammed into me as she carried it down the platform. She was running, headed toward a small fence at the far end.

"Nazuna! Get back here!!"

The woman continued shouting as she and the man passed in front of me...

Who is that guy anyway?

The heavy suitcase and unfamiliar shoes seemed to slow Nazuna down. Before she could even reach the fence, her mother and the man had caught her easily.

My body felt frozen in place. I could do nothing but watch.

"Nazuna! What were you thinking?!!"

Nazuna struggled with all her might, desperate to break her mother's hold.

"Stop it! Let me *go*!! Stop it!!"

"Honestly, get ahold of yourself! Why are you always so difficult?!"

"Shut *up*! Let me go! Get your hands off me!!"

Finally, Nazuna seemed to have either drained all her strength or accepted her fate. Her mother and the man each gripped one upper arm and began pulling her in my direction.

"Norimichi! Help me!!"

"!!"

I jolted at Nazuna's imploring use of my first name—and

again at the subsequent glare I received from her mother. Every muscle in me went stiff.

Nazuna kept screaming as the two adults continued to drag her toward the ticket gate.

"No! I won't go! I don't want to go!!"

This scene, these voices... I've been through this before.

The only differences were the place and...the first time, the man hadn't been around. It had been just Nazuna and her mother...

Wait... The first time? When was that?

My mind was getting even more mixed up. The only thing I was sure of was that I had definitely seen this happen before.

"Don't touch me! Let me go!!"

Nazuna tried to shake the man off her right arm as she screamed. The orb she'd been holding in that hand sailed into the air.

"Norimichi! Help!! Norimichi!!"

Nazuna's tear-streaked face had turned toward me. The orb was falling to the ground in slow motion. The instant it hit the rough, graveled surface of the platform, I burst into a run.

I won't let them take her!!

The first time—whenever that was—I hadn't been able to do anything. I'd stood and watched as Nazuna was taken away.

But this time...I won't let them! I have to get her back!!

I caught up with them just as they reached the ticket gate. Without thinking, I seized the man's arm.

"What do you think you're doing, kid?!"

"Let her go!"

I pulled as hard as I could, but his firm, muscled limb wouldn't budge. The man jerked his arm, trying to shake me off. His elbow slammed into my cheek.

"Ow!"

Stunned by the blow, I released my grip and crumpled to the ground.

"Geez, kid."

The man stared down at me. I thought I detected the flicker of a smile at the corners of his mouth.

"Norimichi!! Norimichi!!"

Nazuna and her voice faded away beyond the ticket gate. Once again, I'd failed to save her...

Once again?

...Yeah, that was right. It seemed to make sense now.

I fell to the ground last time, too. Just like this...

No, wait... Yusuke was the one on the ground... And I wasn't the one who was hit in the face... I punched Yusuke. But when did that happen? I looked at my right hand—the one that supposedly punched Yusuke. Just beyond my fingers lay the orb.

When I scooped it up, it was cold, like any ordinary hunk of rock. Even so, I felt the tangled threads of my two memories loosen just a bit.

When we'd had the fifty-meter race at the pool, I had lost. I'd injured my foot and run into Nazuna at the hospital. Then, at the fork in the road, Nazuna had been taken away...

And this orb... That's right. After that, I threw this orb.

"Back there... If... If only I'd..."

How had it gone? I'd taken the orb and thrown it while thinking of something, hadn't I? Then, after I threw it...the strangest thing had happened... I'd started living the same day over again, but slightly differently...

Whoosh!

The train at the platform closed its doors. I was tugged back into reality.

Slowly resuming its same old *click-clack* rhythm, the worn-out, one-car train departed.

I watched it gradually recede into the distance. Nazuna's words again floated to mind.

"How about Tokyo? Or Osaka? Anywhere's fine with me. But the farther away, the better."

If… If only…Nazuna's mother had arrived at the station just a little later… Then Nazuna and I would have been on that train, right?

A crow circling high above called out, as if pitying my lonesome figure on the Moshimo Station platform.

My check ached where the man's elbow had connected.

There was no reason for me to be at the station anymore, and I'd begun pushing my bicycle along an unpaved country road. The sun was setting, and the sky along the ridgeline was dyed a deep ochre.

The orb was in my pocket. It didn't seem right to just throw it away, so I'd decided to hang on to it for now.

When I approached an intersection, I heard a troublingly familiar voice come from the crossing farm road.

"The display's gonna start soon, you know."

"We're still not even *close* yet."

"Just shut up and walk!"

Kazuhiro, carrying a huge backpack on his shoulders, was shouting at Junichi and Minoru behind him.

Oh yeah… The farm road's the quickest way from the shrine to the lighthouse…

Junichi noticed my figure and began jogging closer.

"Huh? Hey, it's Norimichi!"

"H-hey, guys…"

"Yo! Norimichi! Where've you been?!"

Kazuhiro and Minoru also closed in on me. Beyond them, Yusuke was standing still, staring at me with hollow eyes.

"Why the crap didn't you come to the shrine?" Junichi said as he lightly kicked my bike.

"Um, well… Something came up…"

I glanced at Yusuke. He was still staring at me. It seemed he hadn't said anything to the others about Nazuna and me…

"So you took care of it and then caught up with us?"

"Huh? Um, yeah, that's right…"

I'd really just run into them accidentally, but when Junichi gave me an opening, I aligned my story to what he'd said.

"Well then, let's keep going. To the lighthouse!"

"Um, yeah…"

"But seriously, I don't even care anymore whether fireworks are round or flat…," Minoru said, munching on some ramen snack mix. He jumped onto the back of my bike.

"Me, neither." Junichi peeled my fingers off the handlebars, hopped on the bike, and started pedaling ahead with Minoru still on the back.

Kazuhiro chased after him, shouting anew.

"Oh, don't even start! Why did we even come all the way out here, then?! Keep walking!!"

Beyond them, up on the mountain, I could see Moshimo Lighthouse and its rotating ray of light. After everything else that had happened, it seemed I'd be heading to the lighthouse with my friends, after all. Just as I'd resigned myself to that fact and begun to follow, a voice came from behind.

"…Where's Nazuna?"

"Huh?"

I turned around in surprise. Yusuke had sneaked up behind me at some point. Up close, I saw a trace of anger in those same empty eyes he'd been watching me with since our paths crossed.

"Oh… She's gone now…"

I considered explaining what had happened at the station but stopped myself. It would just complicate matters further.

"So tell me, why did Nazuna show up at your house in the first place?"

Yusuke seemed to have grown even more irritated, thanks to my ambiguous response. His latest question carried an edge. Part of me wanted to resolve the misunderstanding, but I was still struggling to separate the two sets of memories I seemed to have. I wasn't sure which of those timelines applied to "now."

"Um, well...that's because...at the pool..."

"Spit it out."

"Um, I can't really explain it very well..."

"Are you two dating?"

I felt like I'd been blindsided. Agitated, I found myself suddenly shouting.

"What?! No, we're not dating! What gave you that idea?!!"

"Then, what's going on?!"

The problem was, I had no idea myself. If I honestly laid out everything that had happened, I was pretty sure it would just make him angrier. After racking my brain, the only words I managed to summon came across like a lame attempt to dodge the question.

"Um...well..."

"...God, just shut up, Norimichi."

He spit out his last remark, then started walking after Junichi and the others. Yusuke and I had been friends for a long time, but I was pretty sure this was the first time he'd ever snapped at me like that.

"Whew! Looks like we just barely made it!"

"Whoa! Look how many people there are!!"

Junichi and Minoru jumped off the bike and started running.

We'd arrived at the seaside hill where Moshimo Lighthouse stood. Only a few minutes remained before the fireworks display was set to begin at seven PM.

We could see Moshimo Beach below. It was bustling with crowds of people and strings of lights formed by the long corridors of vendors' stalls. We could see the dim silhouette of Moshimo Island poking out right in the middle of the bay. The dark outlines of several people were swarming about the island like ants. They must have been the fireworks crew.

Just as Kazuhiro had asserted in the classroom, the hill we were on appeared to be perfectly to the side of where the fireworks would be launched.

"So which are they?! Round?! Flat?!" Minoru's voice was a mixture of excitement and exhaustion.

"They haven't even started yet. And they're gonna be round anyway," Kazuhiro shot back, full of confidence.

Junichi's reply came equally fast. "If they're flat, though, we're serious about the homework. All of it... Hey, and since we're here anyway, how 'bout we watch from up there?"

"You mean up on the lighthouse?"

Junichi was pointing a finger toward the slowly rotating beam of Moshimo Lighthouse.

"Yeah! That sounds awesome!"

Minoru approached the base of the lighthouse and tugged on the handle of a small door, which was only about three feet tall. It opened easily but with a drawn-out metallic screech.

"Whoa! Cool! There's a staircase!! Come check it out, guys!"

Minoru, still staring inside, waved us closer with a hand stretched out behind his back.

"Oh, sweet! Think we can go in? Kinda scary in there."

Despite any hesitation he might have been feeling, Junichi's voice was also full of excitement.

I peered through the door from behind Junichi. A spiral staircase wound through the dim light of the interior. I'd been to the lighthouse several times—my first visit was on a field trip all the way back in kindergarten—but this was the first time I'd ever seen the inside.

"Are you sure it's okay? It says NO UNAUTHORIZED ENTRY."
Kazuhiro was looking at a metal sign attached to the side of the
door.

"It's fine! And anyway, it's not like anybody's unauthorized
us! Come on, let's go!"

Junichi's logic was questionable—it was clearly a matter of
needing to be *authorized*, not the other way around. But before
anyone had a chance to call him out on it, we were already starting to file inside the door.

The spiral staircase was punctuated at regular intervals by
bluish-white emergency lamps. It was narrow enough that we
would have to ascend in single file.

"Hey, Kazuhiro! You be in front!"

"Why?!"

"'Cause you've got the flashlight!"

Even though Junichi had been the first to walk inside, he
was already chickening out. He pushed Kazuhiro forward, and
we began a gradual ascent with Kazuhiro in front, then Junichi,
Minoru, me, and Yusuke in back.

Kazuhiro's flashlight revealed a stairway full of cobwebs.
Everything looked eerie, straight out of a horror movie.

"This is seriously giving me the creeps," Kazuhiro whim-
pered as he brushed away the sticky threads with his hand.

While it was true we had a lighthouse in Moshimo, it wasn't
spectacular enough to draw attention on a national scale. It was
about fifty feet from bottom to top, and climbing it shouldn't have
taken more than a minute.

But Kazuhiro's feet weren't moving forward at all.

"Come on, just go! The fireworks are gonna start!"

Junichi was becoming irritated. He pushed at Kazuhiro's
back.

"I know they—!!"

Fyuuu... Boom! Boom-boom!!

The tail end of Kazuhiro's reply was drowned out by a sudden cacophony from outside.

"Oh no!"

"They've started!!"

"Go! Go!!"

With Junichi still pushing him from behind, Kazuhiro seemed to break through his uncertainty. He started charging up the staircase, flailing his light and screaming out a war cry: "Ahhhhhh!" Cobwebs clung all over his body as he made his way to the top.

"Yeah!"

"Here we go!!"

Junichi and Minoru dashed up just behind him.

"Are they round?! Flat?!"

"I keep telling you, they're gonna be round!!"

"You don't know that!!"

Yusuke and I seemed to have missed the cue; we found ourselves alone near the bottom of the staircase. Yusuke refused to look in my direction anymore, and he'd been staying out of any conversations among the other three.

"Let's go…," I said without turning around.

There was no response. I brushed it off and started climbing.

"…Hey!"

I was two or three steps up when Yusuke's voice rang out from behind.

I turned. He glared into my eyes, causing me to flinch.

"…Yeah?"

For whatever reason, I felt like if he saw my fear, he'd win at some unspoken competition we were having. I tried to respond as confidently as I could, but Yusuke's follow-up was even louder.

"…As soon as summer's over, I'm gonna ask her out!"

"Huh?"

"When second term starts, I'm gonna tell Nazuna that I like her!"

As Yusuke made his declaration, he shoved past me and began running up the spiral staircase.

What's his deal...?

I didn't know how to respond, so I just followed him up the stairs.

At the cramped landing at the top, Junichi and the others had encountered an obstacle.

"It won't open! What gives?!"

"You gotta push harder!"

The door leading outside was rusted shut. We could hear the explosions of the fireworks on the other side. The sounds were coming closer and closer together.

"Hurry up and open it! The show's gonna be over!" Kazuhiro was frantic.

"Oh, come on. It *just* started! ...Okay, let's all push at the same time."

Junichi shoved his sleeves up to his shoulders.

"On three! Ready? ...Come on, get over here!"

"R–ready..."

Caught up in his enthusiasm, we all crammed ourselves in front of the door.

"Here we go... One...two...three!!"

At Junichi's signal, all five of us threw our weight against the door.

Slam!!

After all the fuss we'd made, it swung open fairly easily— leaving us all collapsed in a big heap under the doorframe.

"Ow..."

"Hey! Get off!"

"Which one of you is on top of me?!!"

Amid our shouts, Junichi was the first to pull himself free and stand. He ran to the railing, leaned over the side, and exclaimed, "Which is it?!"

Minoru and Kazuhiro were next. They lined up beside Juni-chi at the railing.

Fyuuu...

I heard the sound of another shot fired and looked intently at the night sky.

"Round or flat?!"

As if in response to Minoru's question, the firework burst open.

Boom! Boom-boom!!

The first firework I'd ever seen from the side...was flat.

"...No way..."

I stared dumbfounded. The dark sky filled with more bursts of color, but every single one was a thin, flat oblong... It was a pathetic imitation of the fireworks I was used to seeing.

"See! They're totally flat!!"

Junichi grinned and gave Minoru a high five. Kazuhiro, on the other hand, was mute with shock.

Junichi and Minoru clung to each other and cheered, "Whoo! No homework for us!"

But to me, their cheers seemed to be coming from some other, faraway place.

It wasn't supposed to matter whether fireworks were round or flat. But for some reason, I just couldn't accept what I was seeing.

Weird. This is weird. Something isn't right.

As I continued to stare, I heard Kazuhiro mumbling to himself.

"This makes no sense! There's no way they should be flat!"

He was right. What we were seeing couldn't possibly be correct. Fireworks...were supposed to be round. A world where fireworks were flat wasn't supposed to exist. Yet, the ones right before my eyes were most certainly flat.

How could this be?

And why had I thought fireworks were round?

"...Impossible. This can't be happening...," Kazuhiro said.

"Impossible. There isn't a world where that can happen."

Kazuhiro's words echoed something I'd heard Yusuke say before.

The two tangled threads of memory I was carrying around jerked themselves free, and finally everything became clear.

"Back there... If only...I'd won..."

That was the thought I'd held in my mind as I hurled the mysterious orb with all my might.

The fork in the road—the fork in my *memory*—had started there.

Everything that had happened must have been caused by that orb Nazuna picked up. And when I'd made my desperate wish... that had been the beginning of the repeated day.

"Yusuke," I started.

I didn't wait for him to respond.

"...I'm gonna get Nazuna back."

Atop the Lighthouse

There's a flash.

   Norimichi is throwing the wishing orb at the fork in the road.

   The area around him is bathed in light, and then it begins to bend and distort into some kind of dimensional void.

   Norimichi's and Nazuna's eyes meet in the pool.

   Norimichi is in his bedroom, talking with Yusuke.

                    YUSUKE
     Seriously, though. Of course fireworks are round.

                    NORIMICHI
     Huh? Really?

                    YUSUKE
     Yeah! Wait a second, you don't really think…?

NORIMICHI
(Embarrassed)
No! I mean, I guess so…

YUSUKE
Are you stupid? In what kind of world
do they have flat fireworks? Think about
it. There's a bunch of powder inside,
and it explodes outward. Of course
they're gonna look round, no matter
what direction you see them from!

NORIMICHI
Yeah, but… What're you gonna do if we
find out they're flat?

YUSUKE
Impossible. There isn't a world where
that can happen.

Time jumps forward.

Norimichi removes the orb from his pocket,
pulls his arm back as far as he can, then hurls
the orb forward, aiming toward the flat fireworks adorning the night sky!

NORIMICHI
If only I'd—!!

The orb glows as it flies through the sky.
Its colors are now strange, unearthly. The area
around it begins to bend and distort into some
kind of dimensional void.

Norimichi, Yusuke, Junichi, and the others
are bathed in light.

ALL
???!!!

"If only I'd gotten on that train with Nazuna!!"

Wishing World 2

I heard the *click-clack* of the train approaching from afar. I raised my voice so I was sure Nazuna could hear me from beyond the bathroom wall.

"Hey, the train's coming!"

"I know. I just finished…"

I turned with my eyes toward the ground, and a pair of bright-red pumps suddenly entered my view. When I looked up, Nazuna was standing before me—a trace of embarrassment on her face.

She was in a black cocktail dress. The neck dipped down far enough to reveal a slight amount of cleavage. Her wavy hair hung around her shoulders, and her lips were faintly red, indicating a trace of makeup.

She was a different person from the Nazuna I'd walked into the station with moments earlier. But at the same time, I felt like I had seen her that way before.

"So? Do I look eighteen? …I do, right?" As if disconcerted by my stare, Nazuna kept looking away as she mumbled her question.

"Uh…well…um…"

I racked my brain but wasn't coming up with any real words.

I had no idea what to do. I merely stood there, whipping through my own thoughts like I was beating an egg in a mixing bowl.

Nazuna, still refusing to look at me, pulled something out of her pocket.

"Look at this."

"Huh?"

Nazuna held out the mysterious orb from before.

"...Yeah, you showed me earlier at the pool..."

"I found it in the ocean this morning. For some reason... when I found this, my mind was set. I decided to leave."

"..."

Nazuna peered at the orb in her hand as she continued.

"No, wait... That's not quite right..."

"It was when I won the race. Right?"

Nazuna lifted her face, clearly startled at how I'd just finished her thought.

But I'd surprised myself even more. The moment I'd seen her in that dress, something had felt strange. At first, I'd thought I was just bewitched by her appearance. But there was something more.

What was strange was that I'd seen it all before.

I'd stood on this lonely platform at Moshimo Station, under this same mix of orange, yellow, and still-just-barely-indigo sky, and I'd seen Nazuna before me, with the orb in her hand. I *remembered* this scenery. I *remembered* having these sensations.

It was that feeling of reliving the same moment over again... déjà...

No, it's not that...

I was pretty sure... No, I was *certain* that I'd stood in that exact spot before. And something was about to happen... Something really bad...

Whoo-whoo!

We heard the sound of the train's whistle.

"Come with me," Nazuna said, gazing right into my eyes.

I looked back. I *knew* those pleading, tear-filled eyes.

"…"

The *click-clack* of the train was now accompanied by the screech of its brakes. The train slid slowly into position alongside the platform.

Soon, it would be completely stopped, and the doors would open.

What was I supposed to do? If I boarded the train with Nazuna, how far away would we go?

I thought as hard as I could, but no answer was forthcoming. I only knew one thing: A premonition so strong it bordered on total conviction was warning me that if we stayed as we were, something bad was going to happen.

"Hey, does this seem familiar to…?"

"Nazuna!!"

A shrill voice emanated from the direction of the ticket gate, ripping apart our shared moment.

That was it. That voice. That was the voice that heralded all the bad things that would happen.

When I turned around, I saw exactly what I thought I would: Nazuna's mother and a middle-aged man running past the ticket gate. They were heading toward us with anger written all over their faces.

Though their expressions surprised me, I wasn't scared. Nazuna dashed for the fence at the end of the platform, slamming into me as she went by.

"Nazuna! Get back here!!"

The woman continued shouting as she and the man passed in front of me. I watched them, trying to figure out what I should do. Next, Nazuna would be…

"Nazuna! What were you thinking?!!"

Before Nazuna could clear the fence, she was caught by her mother.

"Stop it! Let me *go*!! Stop it!!"

The girl struggled desperately, but it was to no avail. Nazuna was pulled back toward the ticket gate, her mother and the man each gripping one upper arm.

I'd seen this entire scene play out before. But even though I realized exactly what was going on, I still found myself unable to move.

"Norimichi! Help me!!"

I heard her voice. I'd heard it however many times before. Last time, I'd remained frozen. But even this time, I still had no idea how to act.

My mind was getting even more mixed up. The only thing I knew was that I had definitely seen this happen before.

"No! I won't go! I don't want to go!!"

Nazuna's voice began to fade as she was dragged away. I had to save her...but my feet wouldn't move, as if they were glued to the ground.

"Don't touch me! Let me go!!"

The voice was getting farther and farther away.

What should I do? I...

"Norimichi! Help!! Norimichi!!"

Nazuna's voice resonated around me, and my head shot up. She tried to shake the man off her right arm, and the sudden movement caused the orb to sail into the air from her hand.

The instant I saw it hit the surface of the platform, I felt as if my body had been released. I burst into a run.

I won't let them take her!!

I caught up with them just as they reached the ticket gate. Without thinking, I seized the man's arm.

"What do you think you're doing, kid?!"

"Let her go!"

I pulled as hard as I could, but his firm, muscled limb wouldn't budge. The man jerked his arm, trying to shake me off.

His elbow... That's it...! Next, the elbow's going to hit me in the face!

I instinctively drew my head back, and the man's elbow sliced through thin air.

When the miss threw him off-balance, I launched myself forward and tackled him. I felt my right shoulder dig into his side.

"Oof!"

The man let out a short yelp, and our tangled bodies both tumbled to the ground. The rough gravel of the platform bit into my left palm. It stung, but I kept pushing firmly against the ground and raised myself back up.

"Nazuna!"

I'd never shouted her first name like that before. But we had no time for delicacy. Nazuna's mother had released her grip in shock after witnessing my scuffle with the man. I saw our chance and reached out my right hand toward Nazuna.

The door of the train began to close.

"Let's go!"

I grabbed her wrist and yanked her to me with all my might. The two of us fell into the train just as the door finished sliding shut.

"Nazuna! Get back here!!"

We could hear her mother's voice from outside, but the train rocked gently and began slowly rumbling out of the station.

By the time we pulled ourselves up from the floor of the railcar, we'd already left the platform. Through the window, we saw the shouting figures of Nazuna's mother and the man slowly shrink into the distance. As they grew smaller, the vast sky filled our view instead. The shade was a bit bluer than when we'd seen it at the station. It would grow dark soon.

I was reminded that it was the night of the fireworks display. Soon I'd be watching the show with Junichi and the others...

No, I'll be watching it with Nazuna... Wait... Huh?

Which was it? Who had I made plans with?

When I tried to pull the events of that day from my memory, my eyes unconsciously shifted downward and landed on the mysterious orb clutched in my left hand.

Huh...? When did I...?

I was sure I'd seen the orb fall onto the platform at the station... Why was it in my hand?

Suddenly, Nazuna's voice cut through the haze of questions clouding my mind.

"That was amazing! Norimichi, I had no idea you knew how to fight like that!"

When I looked over, I found that Nazuna had sat down on one of the car's benches.

"Oh, um, I think it was really just momentum... Hey, who was that guy anyway?"

"Hmm? He's my mom's new fiancé."

"Huh?"

She'd said it casually, but from the way she averted her gaze as she spoke, I suspected that her feelings toward the man were complicated.

"Oh, I see..." Was I supposed to ask more about the man? Was I supposed to change the subject? I'd inadvertently unearthed another small question that was now squirming around in my mind.

"Anyway, come have a seat. We've got the whole place to ourselves." Nazuna patted an adjacent space on the red-upholstered seats.

I looked around the narrow railcar. We were the only two there.

I felt a little embarrassed to just sit down at her invitation, but a moment later, the train happened to go into a short tunnel. I took advantage of the momentary darkness and sat next to Nazuna—or more precisely, on the same bench about two feet away.

"My mom says she's going to get remarried."

When we came back out of the tunnel, I was surprised to find her closer to me than I'd expected. She faced forward as she spoke. I started to lift myself up, intending to scoot a little farther away, but just then Nazuna scooted in toward me.

"Can you believe it?! It'll be her third time!"

I dropped my weight back down in the seat, searching for something to say but unable to come up with anything worthwhile.

"...Huh. I had no idea..."

In truth, I did know that Nazuna's mother had been remarried. Nazuna's dad had been the second husband—before his death.

"The first time my mom was married, she started having an affair. That was with my dad. But when she got pregnant with me, the two of them decided to elope. It sounds like something out of a soap opera or a movie. That means I'm the daughter of a forbidden romance. Pretty cool, huh?"

It felt like Nazuna was intentionally trying to sound light-hearted as she talked about that cheerless episode. I tried to play along, keeping my responses casual. Inside, however, I felt dejected.

Right after Nazuna had moved to Moshimo, I'd overheard my mom and dad talking about Nazuna's mother. My mom had said something with a disapproving look on her face: *"She's fickle, that woman."* For whatever reason, those words had stuck with me ever since.

I didn't understand what *fickle* was supposed to mean at the time, and honestly, I still didn't have a good grasp of what my mom had wanted to say.

But after Nazuna's dad passed away, her mother started

working at a bar. I'd heard people say she was popular among the men around town, and I figured her being "fickle" probably had something to do with it.

"But then my dad died." Nazuna's next words came a little heavier.

Her father had died in the summer of last year.

A while after the tsunami, the surfers who had stopped coming to Moshimo Beach had started to trickle back in small numbers. Business had picked up again at the surf shop Nazuna's dad ran.

Around that time, one inexperienced surfer vacationing from Tokyo had been swept out to sea. Nazuna's father had swum out to rescue him but got caught in the surf himself. Both drowned. The tidal currents around the Moshimo coast were strong. Two days later, in the morning, the body of Nazuna's father washed up on the shore.

I remembered that day, too. My own mom and dad had been in a harried state all morning. Finally, my dad had run out of the house, heading toward the beach. I'd followed.

A huge crowd had assembled there. On the sand was a blue tarp with a small lump in the center. Nazuna and her mother had clung to the tarp, both sobbing.

Nazuna had knelt facing her father's remains as she wailed, oblivious to the soaking waves rolling up around her. She was clutching the tarp so tightly that her hands had gone completely white. Even from where I was standing, I could see those hands clearly.

"It hasn't even been a year since then, and already she's with a new man... It's unbelievable..."

Nazuna's hands were clenched tight, just like that day.

Her head was down, so I couldn't see her expression. But the exchange put to rest a number of the questions writhing in my brain. It seemed Nazuna wasn't happy with the new fiancé and didn't want him living in her home, and that was why she wanted to leave.

"...So that's why you decided to run away?"

I turned to face her, but her head remained down, and no reply came.

"I'm right, aren't I?" I said.

At that, Nazuna popped out of her seat. She stared down at me as she said, "Could you stop calling it that? 'Running away' sounds so kiddish."

Her sudden movement had caught me off guard, but I tried to hide my surprise with a casual response.

"Then what is it?"

Nazuna leaned in toward me and brought her index finger right in front of my nose.

"E-lo-ping."

"Huh?!"

"You and me. We're eloping. My mom's a slut, and that makes me one, too. I've got her blood."

"..."

I felt my cheeks burn in the face of her overpowering smile. Realizing how I must have looked, and not wanting her to notice, I tried to steer the conversation elsewhere.

"...Yeah, and what're we gonna do now?"

Huh?

My choice of words startled me. Had I come off sounding like I was on board with Nazuna's "e-lope-ing" plan?!

Whoa, whoa, whoa. I don't want to elope. I'm still in seventh grade! It's summer vacation! I still have homework to do, and...

My brain was spinning, but Nazuna was still there, her piercing eyes staring straight into mine.

"Just like I said. We'll go to Tokyo, and we'll start a life there together."

"Huh?"

"If I can't find a place at a nightclub, maybe I'll try being a singer."

"Are you *serious*?"

I let out a laugh. Nazuna, as usual, didn't give the slightest hint as to whether she was joking or not. Her lips formed her usual subtle, mysterious smile.

"You don't think so? I bet I've got what it takes."

Nazuna suddenly straightened her back, closed her eyes, and drew in a deep breath.

"Every night must come to dawn; the sun will surely rise,"
Wistfully, you sighed to me back then

Huh? Now she was *singing*?

It was a song I'd never heard before. Her sudden performance made me anxious. Even though I knew we were all alone on the train, I began furtively glancing around the interior of the car.

Nazuna kept on singing, unaware of and unconcerned by my embarrassment.

The lighthouse stood behind us as we watched the bay
Our eyes filled with the endless dark of the sea

Her eyes slowly reopened and again stared at me. Flustered by her gaze, I tried to break her off before she began singing the next lines.

"Hey! Um... What... What was that?"

"My mom always sings this at karaoke. It's by some lady named Seiko Matsuda. I've heard it so many times since I was little that I know it all by heart."

Though she'd briefly gone back to normal and humored my question, as soon as she'd answered it, she resumed singing.

Troubled times, they come and go
And some days hope feels thin
But I know that all is not so bleak
Always your hand reaches out and comforts me

Lends me strength
To carry on

I had a whole slew of other questions I wanted to fire off at her. Why'd she suddenly start singing? Why this song? But as Nazuna's voice rose with each line, I found myself entranced by the melody and lyrics.

The sunlight shining through the windows of the train car had weakened, but it seemed to provide a spotlight especially for Nazuna. Our worn-out little train had been transformed into a stage for this girl and her audience of one.

When the morning sun breaks from the horizon
Rays of light will streak across the sky

Far in the distance, the evening sun was sinking into the sea beyond Moshimo. It wasn't the dawn, but its rays truly did appear to streak across the water and the sky.

Together, we will see once more around us
Our shining, lapis-colored earth

Having sung that much, Nazuna seemed satisfied and sat back down beside me.

I didn't know exactly what kind of color lapis was, but when I looked outside, the sky was slowly growing bluer and bluer in contrast to the orange of the setting sun. It occurred to me that the color she'd been singing about might be the color I was seeing in the sky.

Lighthouse, sea, rays of light, together... The words from her song seemed to symbolize all the things that had happened around me that day.

There was the lighthouse I'd said I'd go to with Junichi and the others, the sea where Nazuna had stood, the rays of light that had shot out from the mysterious orb, and the extra chances I'd been given to be together with Nazuna...the wishing worlds we'd been able to visit.

Vague though the realization was, I understood now.

Twice in the past, I'd fervently wished that some event could have gone differently. As I'd done so, I'd thrown the mysterious orb that was currently in my left hand. And after each throw, I'd been transported to the point in time I'd wished to change. In other words, this orb—this wishing orb—seemed to have created each new world. It seemed to be the source of the strange phenomenon occurring around me.

But if that was so, what exactly was this strange wishing orb that Nazuna had picked up from the sea? I'd never been a fan of sci-fi stuff. I didn't read those kinds of novels or watch those kinds of movies or cartoons. I didn't care for plots featuring time travel or males and females swapping bodies. But I felt like the things I was experiencing might be akin to those kinds of stories.

But this isn't a story... This is real...

Or was I even certain of that? What if this was all just a long, drawn-out dream? At some point I might wake up and head to the bathroom like I always did in the morning. Then my mom would snap at me, *Hurry up and eat your breakfast!* And I'd do that. Then I'd ride my worn-out bike down the slope, racing to school with Yusuke, Junichi, and Minoru. And when we got to the boardwalk...I'd catch sight of Nazuna standing at the water's edge...

That's right. Maybe what started this whole, strange day was the moment Nazuna picked up the wishing orb on the beach.

First, Nazuna had picked it up, and then it had rolled to my hand during the encounter at the fork in the road. I'd used it, beginning the first wishing world, and the orb had gone back to Nazuna. The next time, when Nazuna had been caught by her mother and the man, the orb again came to me. That led to the second wishing world... But even though the orb had gone back to Nazuna...later it had shown up in my left hand.

And anyway, why had Nazuna been walking out by the water in the first place?

"I know we can't really do it. Elope, I mean…," Nazuna murmured, pulling me back to the moment.

Since we'd boarded the train, her mood had risen and fallen dramatically, to the point of bursting into song. I felt like I was hearing her normal voice for the first time in a while.

"But before I move away… Before summer vacation is over…"

Huh? Move away…?

I felt a big *thump* in my chest, as if my heart had caused my entire body to jolt.

Even before we'd boarded the train, people's moods had been fluctuating up and down around me all day, filling me with surprise and confusion. But the words *move away* coming from Nazuna hit me with a whole different kind of impact. It made my heart jump into my throat.

My entire day—from morning until now—had been nothing but surreal experiences. I didn't know whether they were real or not. But at least I'd been able to see them all with my own two eyes.

Nazuna moving away, on the other hand, felt intangible. It seemed like an impossible future.

I mean, if she moved away, she wouldn't be in Moshimo any longer…

The girl sitting right next to me now… I won't be able to see her anymore…

So that was the significance behind her mother's remarrying: The newlywed couple was planning to move out of town and take Nazuna with them. The logic was simple enough, but until then, the thought hadn't even occurred to me. I'd never lived anywhere other than Moshimo during my entire life. Where else was there to be? I'd assumed that even if Nazuna's mother did remarry, or even if the new fiancé was someone Nazuna didn't like, Nazuna herself would obviously always be here in Moshimo.

"Huh? Move away…?" I managed to squeeze the words out.

They were so soft and hoarse, I wasn't even sure she had heard them.

Her head was slumped forward, but she bobbed it slightly up and down.

"That's why…before I do, and while it's still summer…just for today…I thought the two of us could…"

The train was approaching a crossing, and the clanging sound of the crossing bells drowned out Nazuna's last few words.

Huh? If the two of us could what…?

I didn't feel like I could ask her to repeat herself. Instead, I clenched down on the wishing orb, still in my left hand.

I'd come to that wishing world in order to get Nazuna back. That's why we'd caught the train. But none of it mattered, because even in that world, Nazuna would ultimately be taken somewhere far away.

My downcast eyes were treated to a view of my old, beat-up sneakers and Nazuna's red pumps…

The bright color burned itself into my eyes.

Clang, clang, clang, clang!

The unsympathetic noise drew closer. The irritation bubbling up in me had no outlet.

Why?! Why did she have to go…?

If her mother wanted to get remarried, she was free to make that choice. But shouldn't she be thinking a little more about how it would affect her daughter…? How cruel, making her leave Moshimo…

No, Nazuna had probably already spoken her mind. She'd probably fought with her mother, saying she didn't want to move. But her mother had ignored it…prompting Nazuna to run away…

But even Nazuna herself had just admitted that a couple of junior high school students like us couldn't really run away or elope… So what choice did we have…? How could we keep Nazuna from having to leave Moshimo?

If... If only... Yes, if only...

When the thought entered my mind, I sensed a curious warmth in my left hand. The orb I'd been clutching was emitting a faint heat. No, it wasn't just heat. Until then, the orb had been black like cast iron. But unless my eyes were playing tricks on me, it seemed to be glowing red as it warmed.

That was the answer...

If... If only...Nazuna's mother didn't get remarried...

No... The thing troubling Nazuna had to be further back. What was it?

...If... If only... That's it...! If only Nazuna's father hadn't d...

"It was at my dad's spot. The place I picked that up."

"Huh?!"

When Nazuna suddenly started talking about her dad, I worried for a moment that she'd seen right into my mind. But her faint, soft smile reassured me that wasn't the case.

"Your dad's spot?"

"The place where my dad...washed up..."

"...Oh."

My mind momentarily flashed back to the scene of Nazuna that morning. I'd thought it strange for her to be out on the beach before school. But her words filled in the blanks, and a distant memory I had about that place returned to mind.

One year ago, I'd seen her clutching at that tarp covering her father's body. It occurred to me that the place where that tarp had been was the same spot on the beach where I'd seen Nazuna crouch down in the morning. That was indeed the place her father's body had washed ashore. To Nazuna, it was the last place she'd been able to be with her dad.

My hand naturally tightened, and I felt a growing warmth again. I didn't know if it was the heat of my own body being transmitted to the orb, or if the orb was generating its own heat. But I did know what I was supposed to do.

I'd throw the orb one more time. Our next wishing world would be a reality where Nazuna's father hadn't died.

The two worlds I'd relived already had been jumps back of just a few hours—or thirty or forty minutes. When I threw the orb this time, I'd be going back a whole year.

A world where a person who was supposed to die survives…

I wasn't sure if it was an acceptable thing to do. And I still didn't know exactly what kind of world Nazuna and I were currently in—what things might have changed.

But I didn't care anymore about things like fireworks. I didn't care whether they were round or flat. I knew what I was supposed to do. For Nazuna, I'd…

I moved the orb from my left hand to my right.

Going back a year meant giving up the three inches I'd grown in height since then. But I'd grow it back.

I clenched my right hand.

Here we go…

"If only…"

I lifted myself out of my seat and began to raise my arm. Just then, Nazuna seemed to notice something outside the window.

"Huh? Yusuke?"

"What?"

Her words caused me to freeze in a farcical, half-finished pose. I stumbled out of it awkwardly, like some kind of slapstick comedian, and then whirled around to face the window. I leaned in close to the glass, thumping a hand against it.

As the train neared the crossing, I saw Yusuke…along with Junichi, Minoru, and Kazuhiro.

On a train anywhere else in Japan, it would have been a fleeting moment. The train would have sped through the crossing, and we'd have been long gone before anyone had time to react. But on the slowly rumbling Moshimo Railway train, we could watch

Yusuke draw near in such clarity that it was as if we were moving in slow motion.

"Crap!"

The moment the train entered the crossing, I tried to sink down below the windows, but the last thing I saw was Yusuke and the others looking up at the windows of the train. Every face was contorted in disbelief.

At the Crossing

The train passes by, the crossing bells fall silent, and the crossing bar lifts up.

Yusuke and the others watch the train slowly roll away.

                    YUSUKE
          …

                    JUNICHI
          Huh? Was that Norimichi just now?

                    KAZUHIRO
          And that was Nazuna with him, right?

                    JUNICHI
          Huh? Yusuke, what's going on? Why's
          Norimichi on a train? And why are the
          two of them together?

                    MINORU
          They're probably dating!

                    JUNICHI
          You think so?!

Junichi and Minoru jokingly embrace each other.

Yusuke is frozen, watching the train recede into the distance.

Then, suddenly…

                         YUSUKE
     …Dammit!

Yusuke starts sprinting along the tracks, chasing after the train.

                        JUNICHI
         Whoa! What are you doing?!!

Junichi, Minoru, and Kazuhiro chase after Yusuke.

I sat on the floor of the train with my back against the seat bottom.

Nazuna laughed at my pitiful figure. "Huh? What's wrong? Why are you making that face?"

My eyes and mouth were both wide open. It was apparently comical to Nazuna, as she began giggling even harder.

For a moment, that laughter made my heart leap. It was good to see her back to her happy, smiling self. But my joy didn't last long.

"Oh, crap, they saw us... They saw me with you..."

"What are you talking about? Does it matter if they saw us?"

"Yeah. Oh man, this is bad..."

"Why?"

"'Cause I told those guys I was gonna watch the fireworks with them today... Well, it's more than that. Yusuke thinks you're..."

"Thinks I'm what? What're you saying?"

"Um...well, I mean..."

Even *I* was unimpressed at how lame I was acting after my earlier heroics. But I really panicked when I heard Yusuke's voice outside the train.

"Norimichi! You better get back here!!"

I hurried to the window at the back of the train car. Outside, Yusuke and the others were running along the tracks after the train. It looked like they were about one hundred feet away...

No matter how slow the rumbling old train was, the legs of a bunch of junior high students were still no match. But when we neared the next station, and the train started to slow...

And why was Yusuke so pissed off anyway?

It's true I'm on a train with Nazuna, but...

I recalled what happened in front of my house. I was supposed to go to Moshimo Shrine with Yusuke, but instead I'd ridden away on my bike with Nazuna sitting on the back... To Yusuke, it must have looked like I was stealing the girl he liked... And now there we were, on a train together. It seemed like a good reason to be pissed off. But on the other hand, it also seemed kind of silly…

This isn't the time! I've gotta figure out what to do!

"Huh? Why are they chasing after us?! This is really creepy!" Nazuna had followed me to the window. She watched Yusuke running after us with murder on his face. She seemed both scared and repulsed.

"Like I was saying…you're someone Yusuke l—"

I started to tell her, but Nazuna looked in another direction and shrieked.

"Huh?! *Mom?!*"

"What?!"

I followed her gaze. On an inland road running parallel to the train tracks, we saw a small car speeding along.

I could make out Nazuna's mother sitting on the passenger side and the man in the driver's seat. The woman was saying something while pointing at the train. I didn't know how to read lips, but I could imagine her words: *"There they are! Drive faster!!"*

"What do we do, Norimichi?!"

Nazuna clasped the sleeve of my T-shirt.

Yusuke was chasing us from behind. The car was alongside us, now driving faster than the train. I tried to think.

Pretty soon, we'd stop at the next station. Yusuke would probably climb up from the tracks onto the platform. The car would get to the station before us, and Nazuna's mother and the man would come in from the ticket gate…

At this rate, we'll be surrounded.

I noticed that the interval between each *click-clack* made by the train was growing larger. We had begun to slow.

"Let's get off…"

"Huh?"

"At the next station. We're getting off the train!!"

Unlike the moment where we'd jumped aboard at Moshimo

Station, this time my resolve came quickly. I took Nazuna's hand and felt its warmth bleed into mine.

No matter what happens next, there's no way I'm letting go of this hand!!

I squeezed more tightly, as if to seal my decision.

Back along the tracks, Yusuke and the others had almost reached the edge of the platform. I saw the small car already parked near the little roundabout at the station entrance. Nazuna's mother and the man were climbing out.

Scree-ee-eeech!

The train slid into Moshimo Lighthouse Station with an ear-splitting whine of its brakes. I knew that the doors wouldn't open until the train had stopped completely. Nonetheless, we waited in front of them anxiously.

Whoosh! The door began to open with a great sigh. Nazuna and I glanced at each other.

"Here we go!"

I jumped through the doorway with Nazuna, her hand still firmly in mine. A shrill cry rang out across the platform: "Nazuna!!"

Nazuna's mother waved off the station attendant, who had tried to stop her at the ticket gate. She was heading toward us with fire in her eyes.

Then, from the direction we'd just come, Yusuke barked as he hoisted himself up on the platform. "Norimichi! You better have a good explanation for this!!"

We were trapped: Nazuna's mother on one side, Yusuke on the other. I could feel Nazuna's hand trembling.

"This way!"

I pulled her along, running straight forward from the doorway. A hedge extended out from the sides of the station building, but it was largely withered, too weak now to fill its role as a fence. We weaved through a gap in the branches and found ourselves on the outside of the station.

"Run!"

I pulled harder on her hand, leaning forward as we dashed toward the sloping road on the far side of the roundabout.

"Okay!" Nazuna's short reply came from behind. It felt like she was agreeing to more than just our flight. I felt a rush of confidence, like I'd become a little bit more of a man.

More shouts came from behind.

"Nazuna! Get back here!!"

"Stop! Norimichi!"

A twinge of unease tarnished my newfound confidence. I pushed myself to run faster.

For one brief moment, I looked back. Nazuna's mother, the fiancé, Yusuke, Junichi, Minoru, and Kazuhiro had tried to follow us through the hedge. But they'd been stopped and now seemed to be arguing with the station attendant.

"Hold it right there! Just what on earth do you think you're doing?!"

"That's my daughter! She's…"

"Our friend just ran off that way!"

"And what were you kids doing on the track?!"

"What? Oh, come on, that was…"

"I'm going to have to call the police!"

This is our chance! I thought. They'd undoubtedly be after us again soon, but the argument would buy us some distance. My heart silently thanked the unknown station attendant as we passed a sign reading MOSHIMO LIGHTHOUSE, 0.3 MILES and began to climb the gently ascending road.

I noticed that the wind whipping through the air now held a slight chill. The orange in the sky had retreated almost completely behind the horizon—all but conquered by the deep indigo.

Soon the fireworks display would begin.

"Hey!"

"What?!"

"Where are we going?!"

"I dunno!"

"Huh?"

"I just told you! I don't know!"

"What kind of answer is that?"

As we continued to run, I caught the faint sound of her laughing softly behind me. We'd had an exchange like this when I rode off with her in front of my house. I hadn't known where I was going then, either.

The sign that had flashed by my eyes earlier popped into mind. If we kept going up this slope, it should take us to Moshimo Lighthouse. It seemed funny. Just as I'd agreed to with Junichi and the others, I was going to the lighthouse, after all. I hadn't meant to come. It was just a peculiar coincidence.

"But, you know..." I spoke up, still facing forward.

"Huh?"

"I... If... Even if you're really going away, you know...I still want to be with you right now!!"

"..."

"..."

It was a once-in-a-lifetime declaration, but I was met with piercing silence. Nazuna didn't say a word. It suddenly felt like an inane, embarrassing thing to have said. And even though I'd scraped up all my courage to say it straight, now she was just letting my words awkwardly hang... How lame could I get?

Crap. I shouldn't have said anything af—

But just then, I felt something different in my left hand. It was still clinging to Nazuna's right. She had released my hand for a moment, then clasped it again—this time with our fingers interlocked.

She squeezed tight. I squeezed back.

It would take more than just petty problems to pull us apart now.

On a Road Heading Toward
the Sea

Nazuna's mother, the man, Yusuke, Junichi, Minoru, and Kazuhiro have lost Norimichi and Nazuna. They crane their necks to look in all directions as they run.

Far away, the wind turbines stand along the ridge of the mountains. Their propellers are at rest.

The sound of fireworks being launched drifts in from the direction of the coast and mingles with the lights and chatter of the festival.

> JUNICHI
> Aww! They've started!

> MINORU
> Are they round or flat?

> KAZUHIRO
> There's no way we can tell from here!

> NAZUNA'S MOTHER
> (To Junichi)

Do you know where those two might
have gone?!

                    JUNICHI
    No idea.

    Out of the crowd appear Mr. Mitsuishi and
Ms. Miura. The two are walking arm in arm. Ms.
Miura is wearing a *yukata*.

                    MR. MITSUISHI
        Huh?

                    MS. MIURA
        What? Oh, shoot!

    Junichi and the others notice the pair.

                    JUNICHI
        Ms. Miura?!

    Ms. Miura quickly shifts a few steps away
from Mr. Mitsuishi.

                    JUNICHI
        Oh man. They really *are* dating!

                    MS. MIURA
        No, we're not!!

        (Trying to change the subject)
        What are you all doing, running
        around like that?!

                    MINORU
        What do you mean? We're going to the
        fireworks sh… Hey! Don't you guys
        still wanna go to the lighthouse?

                    MS. MIURA
        L-lighthouse?

JUNICHI
That's right! We have to go find out!

Yusuke, silent up until that point, reacts to Minoru's mention of the word *lighthouse*.

YUSUKE
...!!

Yusuke begins to run back in the direction they've come from.

KAZUHIRO
Hey! Where are you going?!

YUSUKE
(While running)
The lighthouse! That's where they went. I'm sure of it!!

JUNICHI
Seriously?!

NAZUNA'S MOTHER
You're sure?

The group takes off after Yusuke. Mr. Mitsuishi and Ms. Miura are left in silence.

MS. MIURA
What on earth? Honestly, those boys...

MR. MITSUISHI
...Huh? Um, Haruko? Was your chest always that small?

MS. MIURA
What?!

MR. MITSUISHI
Uh, by small, I mean, like, were they always kind of...flat like that?

Mr. Mitsuishi reaches out to check Ms. Miura's chest.

                    MS. MIURA
          What do you think you're doing, you
          pervert?!

Ms. Miura slaps Mr. Mitsuishi.

When we reached the top of the slope, the view suddenly expanded before us. The whole beach was visible from the seaside hill where the lighthouse stood. We could see the lights of the vendor stalls set up on the beach for the show and the silhouettes of people passing between them.

Moshimo Island poked out from the inky water. Faint lights on the island illuminated the dark figures of what must have been the fireworks crew.

It seemed they hadn't started shooting them off yet.

We'd run the whole way from the station and were both out of breath, but we appeared to have shaken off Nazuna's mother, Yusuke, and the rest of our pursuers. Our ragged breathing was the only sound across the dim hill.

We could have let go of each other's hands at that point, but neither Nazuna nor I made any motion to do so. I, at least, didn't want to.

Nazuna's breathing slowly steadied, and she raised her head.

"Looks like we came, after all."

"Huh?"

"To see the fireworks display. We're a little far away, but still..."

"Oh... Yeah, I guess that's right."

I'd been preoccupied with my relief that no one else was around, and after everything I'd gone through that day, the fireworks date was the furthest thing from my mind. Nazuna seemed to have forgotten about it until then, too. We looked at each other and chuckled.

"Well, since we're here, wanna see it from the top?"

"The top?"

I pointed to the lighthouse.

"Huh? The lighthouse? There's a way to get up there?"

"Yeah."

I neared the base of the lighthouse, still guiding Nazuna by the hand.

I put my other hand against the small door there and pushed. It opened easily but with a drawn-out metallic screech.

Nazuna hesitantly peered inside.

"Oh, there's a staircase!"

"It's a little dark, but it'll take us all the way to the top."

"How do you know all this? Have you been inside before?"

"Yeah, I think I have."

"Do you think it's okay? The sign says No Unauthorized Entry."

"Yeah, it's fine. I mean, it's not like we're unauthorized."

"What kind of answer is that? That doesn't even make any sense!" Nazuna laughed as she responded.

Our hands still clasped, we went through the doorway. The spiral staircase was punctuated at regular intervals by bluish-white emergency lamps. It was narrow enough that we would have to ascend in single file. Nazuna stayed close behind me and matched my pace.

Each time she exhaled, her breath ran across the back of my neck. It was a rush, and it gave me the chills.

From outside the walls, we heard a whistling...then: *Boom! Boom-boom!!*

"That's..."

"The show's started."

"Sounds like it."

"Hey, Norimichi..."

"Yeah?"

"Are fireworks round? Or are they flat?"

"Huh?"

"Today, you guys were talking about it in the classroom. Remember?"

"Oh yeah. I guess we were..."

Only four or five hours had passed since then, but it felt like much longer to me—probably because I'd been going back and forth between the same set of hours over and over.

"Well...of course they're gonna be round."

"Really?"

Looking back, I had no idea why any of them had been so worked up over an argument about something so obvious. Just like Kazuhiro had said, it was a bunch of powder that exploded outward. It'd look round no matter which direction you saw it from.

A while ago... Well, my mind was so mixed up by that point, I didn't know exactly when it had happened anymore...but I'd been here with Yusuke and all of them at the top of the lighthouse, and the fireworks we'd seen were flat. But that hadn't been right. There wasn't a world where that could happen. That's why I'd returned to get Nazuna back.

This world was the right one, where Nazuna and I were together, hand in hand. And that meant the fireworks...

"I'm sure of it. They're definitely round."

We arrived at the cramped landing at the top of the spiral staircase. We could hear the explosions of the fireworks on the other side of the door leading outside. The sounds were coming closer and closer together. I recalled that last time, the door had been rusted shut.

I didn't want to let go of Nazuna's hand, feeling like doing so would somehow imply our separation. But I'd need both hands to get the door open. I untangled my fingers from hers, took a firm grip on the handle, and threw all my weight against the door.

It swung wide-open and sent me sprawling outward.

"Whoa!"

I stumbled forward uncontrollably but instinctively grabbed hold of the railing in front of me. The reaction enabled me to steady myself.

"Are you okay?"

"Uh, yeah. I'm good."

Another whistle came from the direction of the beach. We simultaneously turned our attention to the sky. The small trail of a firework streaked straight upward.

A few seconds later, we'd hear it explode and see the big, round shape bloom in the sky. I was sure of it...

Full of confidence, I lifted myself up on the railing. Nazuna was standing to my side. Out of nowhere, I suddenly felt a surge of desire to see what kind of expression she wore as she saw a firework explode. I furtively glanced toward her.

She stood with her eyes transfixed on the sky in front of us. It seemed that even the darkness of night couldn't hide her radiance. I felt captivated anew by that resilient beauty.

I was also overcome with anxiety. How much time did I have left with her...? The hopes and fears in my mind wrestled endlessly.

Boom! Boom-boom!!

The firework exploded. I saw it reflect across her eye: a beautiful flower bursting forth in her dark irises... Except...something was wrong.

"What...?"

Nazuna was the first to murmur in response.

"Huh?"

I hastily flicked my eyes away from her face and back to the sky... The firework spreading out before us was a shape I'd never seen before: a formless mass worming out in every direction...

What in the world is this...?

There were sparks of all sizes, moving around at different speeds and in different directions through the night sky. They squirmed and wriggled as if the firework had a mind of its own... like a living organism writhing across the sky.

It was neither round nor flat. It was a weird, grotesque shape.

"What...? What is this?"

"It's really...yucky..."

Nazuna was right. The fireworks weren't pretty. They weren't beautiful. The only thing they made me feel was a sickening sensation.

Is it some newly developed kind? Do modern shows use grotesque-looking, writhing fireworks like this...?

I tried to rationalize what I was seeing, but the explosions continued one after another. Every firework was the same: not round, not flat...but like some gross amoeba under a microscope.

"Nazuna..."

"Huh?"

"It's not right... This world we're in. It isn't the right one..."

The first time I'd thrown the mysterious orb, I'd come with Yusuke to the lighthouse, and the fireworks we'd seen had been...

Fireworks in that world had been flat. I'd seen them and sensed that wasn't the way things were supposed to be. So I'd thrown the orb again. The fireworks I was seeing now with Nazuna were supposed to be round... They *had* to be round.

We were supposed to be back in the normal world. The *right* world. The world where fireworks were round.

"Fireworks aren't supposed to look like this..."

It was all I could manage to say as we continued to stare at the grotesque shapes spreading across the sky.

I'd been able to get Nazuna back, like I'd wished for in the previous world. But these weird fireworks seemed to be mocking me, telling me I hadn't really accomplished my goal.

Did this mean that the actions I'd taken were wrong? Was this moment shared with Nazuna not meant to be?

I felt something brush against the fingers of my left hand. I looked down and saw both of Nazuna's hands reaching for mine. My hand had been hanging limply at my side. Nazuna softly enclosed it.

"I don't care..."

"Huh?"

"If they're round, or flat, or weird like this."

"…"

Nazuna had been looking down at my hand as she held it. She raised her eyes, and reflected in them was my frustrated expression.

She fixed her eyes firmly on mine and whispered, "If it means I can be together with you, then I don't care how they look…"

There was no trace of hesitation in those eyes.

I felt like I should say something and searched for the right words, but I failed to come up with anything. It felt like Nazuna's eyes would draw me in and sweep me away to another place.

The corners of Nazuna's lips rose slightly.

I felt the muscles of my own face relax, too. We continued staring at each other, smiles on our faces.

Nazuna might not have felt like the world we were in was strange. Maybe I was the only one who was aware of its peculiarity. But her words told me it didn't matter anymore.

As long as I can be with her, even this strange world is—

Just as the thought occurred to me, we heard a shout.

"They're here!"

A voice I'd heard before ripped through the moment we shared.

I leaned out over the railing and peered below. A line of people was heading toward us. Junichi was at its head, with the rest of my friends, Nazuna's mother, and the man trailing behind. They had reached the top of the slope and were now running across the hill toward the lighthouse.

Immediately behind Junichi was Yusuke, who was glaring in our direction.

"What are you two doing?!"

"Nazuna!!"

Kazuhiro's shout and Nazuna's mother's shrill cry came in chorus.

"Nazuna! What on earth are you doing?! Get down from there!!" the woman continued.

I'd heard that voice over and over during the day, but it seemed to have reached a new, frantic peak.

"Hey! Norimichi!!"

"What are you doing up there?!!"

"Nazuna!!"

"Get down here! It's not safe up there!!"

"How'd you guys even get up there?!!"

"Guys, look! The door over here's open!"

A flurry of voices intertwined. I wasn't sure who was saying what, but I knew the last voice had been Minoru's. He was at the base of the lighthouse, pulling on the door we'd left half-ajar. He peered inside.

"Hey! There's a staircase!"

Yusuke's reaction to Minoru's discovery was immediate.

He'd been watching Nazuna and me as he stood slightly apart from Junichi and the others. He turned toward the door and broke into a run. Nazuna's mother wasn't far behind. I saw the two disappear into the lighthouse.

"Yusuke, wait up!!"

Junichi, the rest of the boys, and the man all began running toward the door, too. The cacophony of angry shouts ended, but it was quickly replaced with the sounds of footsteps racing up the spiral staircase—and growing closer.

"What do we do…? Norimichi, what are we going to do…?" Nazuna's unease spilled out.

"…"

Dammit. So even in this world, things end the same.

It didn't matter whether the fireworks were round, flat, or just plain weird. In none of the worlds were Nazuna and I able to be together. It was obvious to me we'd never be able to run away or elope. At most, we could have this one day together... Eventually, I'd have to go home, and Nazuna would have to...

Can't we at least be together until the end of the fireworks display...?!

If only my eyes hadn't met Yusuke's when the train rolled through the crossing... If only Nazuna's mother hadn't been chasing us in her car... If only, if only things hadn't been like that...!!

"Nazuna... Let's go to a world where we can be alone."

As I spoke, I pulled the wishing orb from my pocket.

"Here I go."

"Huh?"

My right hand clenched the orb hard. My left clasped Nazuna's fingers.

This time, I'd take us to a world where it'd just be the two of us.

"If... If only..."

Another grotesque firework bloomed in the night sky. I aimed straight for it, pulling my right arm back behind my head.

"If only! If only Yusuke and Nazuna's mo—"

Slam!

Just as the wishing orb flew from my hand, the door behind us swung wide open.

"Norimichi!!"

Yusuke jumped through and slammed into the two of us full force.

"!!!"

The shock of Yusuke's body sent Nazuna and me flailing forward. I reached my right hand out, trying to grab on to the railing, but the momentum carried us too far forward. My hand closed around nothing but air.

"Oh no..."

The world spun around me. In the next moment, I was in a free fall.

Nazuna and I were still linked, clinging to each other's hands.

We were headed straight for the stretch of ocean just below the lighthouse...

Ahhhhh!! Are we gonna die?! Are we going to fall into the ocean and die?!

The jet-black ocean rushed closer at blinding speed.

I pulled my face upward, resisting the inevitable. My eyes caught sight of the orb—it was still flying straight toward the firework.

I remembered that I'd begun my wish, and I shouted out with every ounce of air in my lungs.

"If only! If only Nazuna and I could be together!!"

Wishing World **3**

When I came to, Nazuna was in front of my face, staring down at me.

"Every night must come to dawn; the sun will surely rise,"
Wistfully, you sighed to me back then

I recognized where I was. *Ah... This part... I'm back here now.*

Unlike my first and second visits to the wishing worlds, in the third world, I felt a clear and immediate sense of having "come back."

The inside of the Moshimo Railway car gently swayed back and forth, keeping time with the *click-clack* of its wheels against the track. From the window, I saw the crimson-tinged sky of early sunset. Nazuna had begun to sing.

It wasn't a nagging sense of familiarity; I knew I had been there before.

"My mom always sings this at karaoke. It's by some lady named Seiko Matsuda. I've heard it so many times since I was little that I know it all by heart."

"...Huh. I had no idea..."

I clearly remembered having given a vague response like that before.

Troubled times, they come and go
And some days hope feels thin
But I know that all is not so bleak
Always your hand reaches out and comforts me
Lends me strength
To carry on

As I listened to Nazuna's song, I thought about what had occurred. The whole situation was like a movie I'd randomly found on TV...

What was the name again? The Girl Who Leapt... *Something like that...*

It was the story of a girl who kept repeating the same day over and over again. I didn't know if that was the kind of thing happening to me. But every time I made a wish and threw the orb...

Huh?

I flexed my left hand and realized something felt different. I looked down to confirm: It was empty. The wishing orb was gone... I felt certain that the last time I'd been on the train with Nazuna, I'd been holding it in my left hand.

Of course, the first and second time I'd gone back, the orb had returned to Nazuna. I looked at her hands, but she wasn't holding anything, either. It wasn't in my pockets. Had it rolled off somewhere? I flitted my gaze around the interior of the railcar but didn't catch sight of anything resembling the orb.

"Hey! Are you listening?"

Nazuna had finished singing and sat back down beside me.

"Um, that, uh...orb from before..."

"Orb?"

"You know, that thing you said you found in the ocean..."

"Oh, that. I think I dropped it just before we got on the train."

"Oh... Is that what happened...?"

I remembered the orb flying from Nazuna's hand when she'd tried to shake the man's grip on her arm. It had seemed to fall to the ground in slow motion, and the instant it hit the rough, graveled surface of the platform, I'd burst into a run.

Then I'd grabbed Nazuna's hand, and we'd jumped onto the train...

Maybe the orb had some kind of limit? Maybe it could only be thrown three times, and only three wishing worlds could be visited. I had no idea how such a rule would have been decided, or by whom, but maybe it was like a pass with a limited number of rides.

If so, did that mean I was stuck in this world? That I couldn't go anywhere else?

"It was at my dad's spot. The place I picked that up."

"Huh?"

"The place where my dad...washed up..."

When she started to talk about her dad, my heart skipped a beat.

It wasn't long after this... Pretty soon we'll...

I strained my ears.

Clang, clang, clang, clang!

The sound of the train crossing was growing louder.

"Get down!"

"Huh? Why?"

"Just do it!"

Nazuna hesitated. I grabbed her by the shoulders and pulled her down with me, so we were both hunched over with our heads against our knees.

"What are you doing?!"

A bit of panic had crept into Nazuna's voice, but I didn't have time to address that now. I prayed for the train to hurry through the crossing.

The clanging of the bells began to die down, replaced by the calm *click-clack* of the train. I lifted myself up and peered out the rear window. My friends were crossing the tracks. I could see

Junichi and Minoru quaking with laughter as they poked fun at Kazuhiro. Yusuke stopped walking for a moment and seemed to look in our direction. But there was no way he could see us from that distance… I felt sure we were okay.

We've cleared Yusuke. The next hurdle is…

"Huh?! *Mom?!*"

Nazuna had noticed a small car running along a road just inland from the train tracks.

I saw Nazuna's mother sitting on the passenger side and the man in the driver's seat. The woman was saying something while pointing at the train. The car picked up speed and started to pull ahead.

"What do we do? …They're going to be waiting for us at the next station. I'm sure of it… They're going to catch us again…"

"No. I think we're gonna be okay…"

"Huh?"

Just then, the train let out an earsplitting whine and began to veer off to the right.

"Whoa!"

"Ahh!"

We both lost our balance. I tumbled to the floor, and Nazuna collapsed onto the seat.

The Moshimo Railway track ran in one nearly straight line from the city to its final stop at Moshimo Station. Yet, the train we were riding had just made a turn almost ninety degrees to the right. The track I knew didn't have any tight curves like that.

The inside of the car continued to sway side to side, but I managed to regain my footing. I looked out the window. The long, straight road where the car had been was receding into the distance. The train was now heading toward the bay—directly through the lines of trees that had been planted along our coast to protect against future tsunamis.

So this is how we avoid capture at the lighthouse station.

With the train veering away from the road, Nazuna's mother would no longer be able to catch us by car. I breathed a sigh. We'd avoided our failure in the previous world. But my relief was soon cut short by Nazuna.

"Norimichi, something's weird…"

Her eyes were wide as she stared out the window.

"What's wrong?"

"Look."

I followed her finger to the lines of trees along the coast.

Our social studies teacher had explained them to us. Moshimo had chosen a species called black pine for the project. Black pine trees grew straight and tall, and they withstood pollution and salty environments well, making them perfectly suited for use as a breakwater. But as if that entire lesson had been a lie, the hundreds of black pines before us now had gnarled, twisted trunks.

It was just like the grotesque fireworks we'd seen in the world before.

"What's going on…?"

"I don't know…" But even as I said it, an inkling of understanding was forming in my mind.

Among the different wishing worlds I'd traversed, I'd encountered flat fireworks, weirdly shaped fireworks, round Watermelon Bars, and wind turbines that spun backward… There had always been something different from the world I'd started out in.

And in this wishing world, too, the scenes and shapes I was used to had changed. Things that were supposed to be round became flat; things that were supposed to be straight were bent and twisted… That must have been why the trunks of the pine trees were gnarled and the usually straight train tracks had bent into a sharp curve.

But if so, then where was this train headed?

As I was pondering the question, the grove of strange trees began to thin.

The train pitched slightly forward, and Nazuna and I experienced a brief moment of weightlessness. Out the front window, beyond the operator's seat, there was nothing in sight but the sea.

"Huh...?"

My weight shifted again as the train leveled out. It continued forward, sliding across the surface of the water as an ice skater might glide across a rink. The familiar, persistent *click-clack* was gone, and the inside of the train was visited by a tranquil silence.

"Is this for real...?"

"...Are we...riding across the surface of the water?"

"...Seems that way."

Moshimo Beach came into view just outside the window.

It was filled with bustling crowds of people waiting for the fireworks to begin. Beyond them were the strings of lights of the vendor stalls. Through the windows on the other side of the car, we could see Moshimo Island rising from the middle of the bay. On it were the figures of what must have been the fireworks crew.

In this world, the train appeared to run along the surface of the water, cutting right through the center of Moshimo Bay...

Does that mean the train is heading for...?

Suddenly, things seemed to click. I thought I understood why the wishing orb was missing from this world. I'd repeated a single day over and over, visiting wishing worlds where one important change had been made. I felt certain we had come to the last of those worlds.

Previously, I'd thrown the orb from the top of the lighthouse. I'd wished *"If only! If only Nazuna and I could be together!!"* That wish had come true. I'd been able to avoid Yusuke and Nazuna's mother, and the two of us were still together at that moment.

But when I'd made that wish, I'd forgotten to add one important detail.

I should have wished instead:

If only! If only Nazuna and I could be together forever*!!*

"What... What's going on...?"

Nazuna stood with her face near the window. She watched the beach roll by.

I approached her and said matter-of-factly, "...It's because I threw that orb."

"Huh?"

"The orb you picked up at your dad's spot."

"...What are you talking about?"

"...If... Just hear me out. If that orb was some kind of wish-granting orb, and if throwing it let you go back to any time or place you wanted...where would you go?"

"That's absurd. Why would it do that?"

"I'm just saying *what if* that was true. What would you do?"

"...How am I supposed to answer a question like that right out of the blue...? I don't know."

"Would you go back to before your dad died?"

"Huh...?"

"I mean, what I'm trying to say is that...I already threw it... earlier..."

"...When?"

"Well, I mean...I threw it a bunch of times."

"...You did?"

"After school, at the fork in the road near your house. When your mom found you and dragged you away."

"...Huh?"

"That was the first time I threw it."

"Hold on a minute. What are you talking about?"

"Don't you remember?"

"No. When did that happen?"

"Today."

"Today?"

"In the evening."

"It's evening right now. And when my mom caught me and was about to drag me away, we were at the station. Just a little while ago."

"No, I'm talking about the first wishing world... I'm trying to tell you. We've been repeating this day over and over. Don't you remember?"

"You're not making any sense. Norimichi, are you feeling okay?"

"It's 'cause I threw that orb..."

"..."

"Do you believe me?"

"..."

"...You're right. This sounds completely insane, doesn't it?"

"...Explain it again. From the beginning."

"Okay... You invited me to the fireworks display because I beat Yusuke when we raced in the pool, right?"

"...That's right."

"But really, I *lost* to Yusuke."

"..."

"At first, you invited Yusuke to go see the fireworks."

"Azumi? Ew. I would never invite him."

"But you did. You invited Yusuke instead of me. And after school, you went to Yusuke's house. But he stood you up, and I ended up going to his house instead... And then, we were walking together, and you got caught by your mom, and I picked up the orb when you dropped it and just hurled it as hard as I could, wishing, 'If only I'd won against Yusuke in the race'... And everything around me started to go all *whoooooosh*..."

"'*Whoooooosh*'?"

"Or maybe not so much *whoooooosh* as like...*nyeeeeeew*..."

"Those aren't even words."

"I'm trying to explain! ...Anyway, so after that, I found myself in the pool again, swimming...and that time I won...and you invited *me*, and so we were gonna go to the fireworks display together...but then..."

"Then *you* stood me up instead?"

"No, I didn't! ...A bunch of stuff happened, but when we were about to get on the train, you were dragged away again. By your mom and her fiancé..."

"And then?"

"And I ended up going to the lighthouse to see the fireworks with Yusuke and the guys. But the fireworks we saw were flat, and...it just wasn't right. Fireworks aren't supposed to be flat. I figured the world I was in was the wrong one, and so I threw the orb again, wishing, 'If only I could have gotten on that train with Nazuna.'"

"...And?"

"And we managed to get on the train, but that time, Yusuke and the others saw us, and your mom was chasing us, too. We ran away from everyone, all the way to the lighthouse... But when the fireworks started, they weren't round—and they weren't flat. They were this super-weird, wiggly shape, and so I figured that world wasn't right, either..."

"So you threw it again?"

"Yeah..."

"What did you wish for that time?"

"Huh? Um...well...I, uh..."

"Say it."

"Uh... Okay, so...I said, 'If only...Nazuna and I...'"

"What? I can't hear you."

"...All right! 'If only Nazuna and I could be together!!'"

"..."

"...That's what I was wishing when I threw it..."

"...And now we're here?"

"...Yeah."

"Well, what about the train? Why's it running over the water?"

"I don't know exactly how it all works, but...in the last world, your mom was waiting for us at the lighthouse station, so..."

"So the train went in a different direction for us?"

"That's what I think... I know it sounds unbelievable...a story like this..."

"...Does that mean you created the world we're in now?"

"No, I didn't exactly create it. It's just that in these, um, wishing worlds, as I keep calling them, things are always a little different than they were before. Like, the fireworks become flat—or weird shaped, I guess. I don't really know..."

"Huh..."

"That's why I was asking you."

"What?"

"If you could go back to some point in time, where would you go?"

"Huh?"

"I mean... I was thinking. The place where you picked that orb up... It was, um... It was the place you last saw your dad, right?"

"Yeah...?"

"The orb came to me, and I ended up throwing it a bunch of times, but...what if that orb was really a gift to you? What if it was from your dad...? I mean, I'm not saying there's, like, a ghost or a spirit hanging around, but, um...what if there's some world beyond our own, where your dad is waiting to reunite with you...?"

"Huh? Are you saying we're being called to the afterworld?"

"No, no, I'm just... How should I put it...? If... *If* that day at the ocean, your dad hadn't..."

"If he hadn't died?"

"…Yeah."

"…"

"…"

"…I wouldn't go back."

"Huh?"

"I miss my dad. I feel lonely now that he's gone, and sometimes I really want to see him again, but…"

"Yeah…?"

"But if I tried to go back to that moment, I think it would make him sad."

"…Why?"

"'Cause I already see him and talk to him, whenever I go to that spot on the beach."

"…"

"Whenever I have some good news or whenever something bad happens, I always go there. I talk to my dad and tell him about everything that's happened."

"…"

"And when I do, I can hear him. My dad's voice floats to me in the sound of the waves, from somewhere beyond the ocean. It always tells me the same thing."

"…What does it say?"

"'Live.'"

"Huh?"

"He says, 'Live.' Just that one word, every time."

"…"

"I heard it this morning, too."

"…"

"That's how I know I'm doing okay."

"…"

"I'm doing okay, Norimichi."

"…"

"...Huh? Are you crying?"

"...I'm not crying."

"You *are*, aren't you?! Look over here!"

"I don't want to!"

"Look at me."

Nazuna grabbed my shoulders and turned me toward her. I didn't know how long the tears had been streaming down my face. Not wanting her to see, I tucked my chin against my chest.

"You know what else...?" Nazuna continued.

"What?" I snapped, a bit defensively.

I wiped my face with the backs of my hands. When I looked at Nazuna, I saw the large droplets that had welled up in the corners of her eyes. Then they were streaming down her cheeks.

"If I went back a whole year, I'd be shorter than you again."

As she cried, she flashed me a radiant smile.

Of all the expressions I'd seen as I'd looked up into Nazuna's face that day, that one was by far the most beautiful.

When the train had cut all the way across Moshimo Bay, it veered again suddenly. The brakes screeched, and our speed fell. We slowly rolled to a stop.

The station we'd arrived at...was Moshimo Station.

In this world, the Moshimo Railway line seemed to run not in a straight line but in a large circle, looping endlessly around the same locations. I'd never ridden on the Yamanote loop in Tokyo, nor had I even seen it in person, but I'd heard about it. Maybe the line we'd just ridden was like a tiny version of the Yamanote Line.

The doors opened, and Nazuna and I stepped out onto the platform.

"We're back where we started."

"Yup."

I scanned the ground, wondering if the wishing orb was lying somewhere nearby. I couldn't see it anywhere.

"Looks like the train can't take us away anymore," Nazuna said.

"Yeah…"

"Because you threw the orb."

"Seems that way…"

I aimlessly looked up at the sky. Just the slightest hint of orange still lingered there among the indigo expanse.

Pretty soon, the fireworks display would begin—the *last* fireworks display of the day.

We headed out from the unmanned ticket gate. Leaning against the station building was my bike. I couldn't help but laugh.

There had been a time when Nazuna and I were on that bike together, riding to the station. I didn't know exactly when it had happened anymore; I just knew that it felt like a long time ago. Back then, I'd had no idea where I was going. I'd just pedaled as hard as I could. But now, neither Yusuke nor Nazuna's mother was chasing us anymore, and the worn-out bike was still there, as if it had been patiently waiting for our return. I stood it up and motioned to Nazuna.

"Shall we?"

"Let's."

We followed the leisurely slope down to the sea. As we rode, we looked around at the strange sights that world had to offer. Like the black pines we'd seen along the coast, the trees growing along the roadside were gnarled and twisted. The walls of the old homes lining the road were not straight but instead bulged outward, like a scene I remembered from a picture book about a house made of gingerbread.

The wind turbines still stood along the mountain ridge, but their propellers now had odd, compounded layers of blades, some spinning vertically and others horizontally. The moon, which hung just above the mishmash assortment of propellers, was a weird, wiggly shape, not unlike the fireworks from the last world.

"Norimichi." Nazuna's voice came from behind.

"What is it?"

"Was this whole world created by you?"

"I dunno. I guess so. Maybe."

"It's like the world in *Alice in Wonderland*."

"What're you talking about?"

"It's like I'm Alice, and you're the White Rabbit. Don't you think so?"

"Huh?"

"Hey, and the White Rabbit threw something, too. Just like you. What was it, again…? A stone? Or some kind of orb?"

I'd heard the title before, and I had some vague idea of what the story was about. But ever since I was old enough to remember, I'd been reading *Shonen Jump* comics. The kinds of books girls read were foreign to me.

"How does that story end?" I asked her.

"Huh?"

"Like, there's a girl named Alice, and she goes to some strange wonderland, right?"

"Obviously."

"Cut it out! I'm trying to ask you how things turn out for Alice."

"…Hmmm, what *did* happen to her? I forgot."

For a while after that, we rode in silence.

Everything we saw in that world seemed strange. But at least one thing hadn't changed: the refreshing ocean breeze that cut its way through the muggy summer air as we rode.

It was the same breeze that had greeted me that morning as I zoomed off from my house and down the slope leading to the sea. As the thought occurred to me, my heart was suddenly stricken with a small, curious fear: Would I never return to what was supposed to be a run-of-the-mill summer day…?

I was enjoying my time with Nazuna, but what would happen to Yusuke and the others, and to my dad, my mom, everyone at school…? Would I never see them again? Would I never again have idle conversations with my friends, or be scolded by my mom, or play at school, or experience that beloved taste of curry left out overnight…?

"Hey, what if…?" Nazuna's voice came from behind. "What if you threw that orb one more time and said you wanted to put things back the way they used to be? What would happen then?"

"Huh?!"

Can Nazuna read my mind in this world?

The idea plagued me for a moment, but I managed to regain my cool and respond. "I guess…the world would go back to how it used to be, wouldn't it?"

"Oh…"

Perhaps Nazuna had been wondering the same things. A moment ago, she'd claimed she couldn't remember what happened to Alice in the end, but based on how those kinds of stories usually went, I doubted the heroine ended up staying in Wonderland forever. I didn't know how things turned out for Alice back in her real world, but it seemed Nazuna was contemplating our own outcome in terms of that story.

If she was right, then when Nazuna went back…

"But if I wished for that…," I began.

"Hmm?"

"That would mean you'd be going away, wouldn't it?"

"…"

"I don't want that… If that's what going back means, then I'd rather stay in this weird world, together with you."

"…"

Nazuna remained silent.

The next words I wanted to say would have felt far too

embarrassing if we'd been standing face-to-face, able to see each other's eyes. But riding together on the bicycle, both facing forward, just maybe I'd be able to get my true feelings out. Maybe I'd be able to entrust my words to the ocean wind whipping by us, and that wind would carry them back to Nazuna's ears.

I tried saying it inside my head once, for practice.

Nazuna... I...

No, I just couldn't get it out! I couldn't make the words come out!!

The bicycle came to the bottom of the slope. When we turned onto the road following the coastline, I finally heard her speak again.

"Hey, how about we go for a swim?"

Following Nazuna's suggestion, I brought us to the far edge of Moshimo Beach.

We walked side by side as we descended the concrete steps leading down from the road. In the twilight, we had to carefully feel our way forward, checking each step with the toes of our shoes.

On the opposite edge of the crescent, we could see the lights of the vendor stalls and the crowds waiting for the fireworks to begin. Nearly the entire population of Moshimo seemed to be gathered there, enjoying the atmosphere.

"Wow. It's true. Nobody comes to watch from this end of the beach."

I couldn't see Nazuna's expression clearly, but her voice was strangely cheerful.

I felt the ground under my sneakers change from concrete to the wood of the boardwalk. I recognized exactly where we were. This was where I'd seen Nazuna at the water's edge... We were standing at the place where she'd last seen her dad.

Mixed in with the bustle from the far edge of the beach was the quiet lapping sound of waves coming ashore.

Nazuna shuffled several steps down the boardwalk and began to take off her shoes.

"You're not seriously going swimming, are you?"

Nazuna ignored me and hopped down from the boardwalk to the sand. When she was a little ways away, she turned in my direction.

Nazuna grabbed the hem of her black dress and slowly began lifting it over her head.

"!!"

Her figure was little more than a shadow. I couldn't see clearly, save for the fact that the color enveloping her body had changed from black to a lustrous silver. It lit up her face ever so slightly, and I saw that she was looking at me—shy and bashful, but smiling.

I didn't know what to do. As I averted my eyes, Nazuna turned away from me and began to run into the sea.

"Hey!!"

I found myself sprinting after her.

She ran in her bare feet. My sneakers sank into the sand with each step. The distance between us grew larger and larger.

Wait!

I started to shout, but my voice was drowned out by the splashing sounds of Nazuna's legs kicking in the water. Eventually, those too faded, and I was left with only the same quiet lapping that had greeted us when we arrived at the water.

I was up to my ankles in water. My sneakers were soaked through. But I didn't care. I was worried about Nazuna, now gone from my sight.

"Hey!! Nazuna!! Are you there?!"

The only thing I could see was the sea, pitch-black like spilled ink, quietly pushing against the shore.

Then, fifty feet out, Nazuna suddenly poked her head from the surface.

"!!"

Her long black hair clung to her face. She didn't bother to pull it away. She stood straight up out of the ocean, looking off in some other direction.

Nazuna's unexpected actions had left my body frozen, but finally I managed to call out, "Don't do anything reckless!"

Nazuna still didn't turn toward me. She looked up at the sky.

"Hey, Norimichi."

"What?"

"What kind of fireworks do you think they have in this world?"

"Huh...?"

"Do you think they'll be round? Or flat? Or some wiggly, weird shape?"

"Umm..."

The distance between us was frustrating. It felt so far from the water's edge to where Nazuna floated out in the sea. I'd been through all those worlds where we had been pulled apart, and I'd rewound just as many times to get her back. At last, I'd found a world where we were alone, but...

No, wait... This might be my chance...

At this distance, where we couldn't see each other's faces, maybe I'd be able to finish saying what I'd tried to on the bike. No, I *had* to say it! Before the first firework went up!

"...Nazuna!"

My voice rang loud enough to surprise even me. Nazuna turned away from the sky to look my way.

"Huh?"

I'd managed to call out to her, and I had her attention, but the next words wouldn't come.

"Um, never mind..."

"What is it?"

Soon the fireworks would start. We'd both look up, curious to know what shape they were. Their sparks would flicker as they fell across the night sky, and there would be light—enough for us to see each other's faces again.

The thing I was trying to say was absolutely, categorically impossible for me to say to her face. I'd gone through the day performing all sorts of acts of courage. Stuff I never could have imagined myself doing. Stuff a hero in a comic book would do. But those actions all paled in comparison to this new task. The stress was on a whole other level.

"What is it? Say it."

Nazuna's tone had grown a bit more forceful.

I have to say it. Here I go. Just say it. Say it!

I waded a little farther into the water, hoping for Nazuna to hear me even a tiny bit more clearly.

"Nazuna! I—"

The whistle of a single, small firework interrupted me. It rose up directly behind Nazuna's back, streaking into the night sky.

"!!"

"!!"

Nazuna and I both followed its course.

From our distance, the pace of the little ball of fire seemed leisurely, and its tail of light wavered as it climbed. Our eyes were pulled up with it, as if they were attached by strings.

It would be the first firework I'd seen *from below* that day.

At long last, the ball of fire slowed and reached its apex. A moment later, the whole sky was filled with one grand explosion.

Boom! Boom-boom!!

The firework spread out in every direction. The sparks drew their arcs across the night at one perfectly uniform speed.

"Wow!!"

"Whoa!!"

It wasn't flat. It wasn't grotesque... It was beautifully, perfectly round.

After that first flourish, the floodgates had opened: New fire-balls streaked up one after another and bloomed into all colors throughout the garden of the sky.

Every one…was round.

For some time, we continued staring up at those round flowers opening up to us… Or rather, I think we were unable to do anything else. But little by little, we were dragged back to reality by the shouts of "Whoa!!" and "Amazing!!" coming from the far edge of the beach.

"Huh? They're…"

"…They're round, Norimichi."

"…How?"

According to the rules of all the wishing worlds so far— Of course, I didn't really know if there were "rules" to begin with… But if there were, the fireworks in this world weren't supposed to be round.

The railway line had curved when it was supposed to be straight. The trees had grown in weird, twisted directions. All sorts of things had been shaped differently than they should have. The fireworks we were watching weren't supposed to be round like in the real world…

Unless this means…

"We've come back…"

"Huh?"

"I think we've come back…to the real world…"

I quickly scanned the ocean and opposite bank. The homes on the mountainside no longer looked like gingerbread houses. They were square and angular as they were supposed to be.

The trees growing around them were standing straight and tall, and the propellers of the wind turbines along the ridge were back to the shape I was accustomed to—even turning clockwise as they always had. And the moon hanging above the turbines… was round.

Did someone else throw the wishing orb?

I felt sure it must have fallen into the sea after I'd thrown it the last time. Then, why had things gone back?

Boom! Boom-boom!! Boom! Boom! Boom-boom!!

Fireworks continued to explode in the sky, as if laughing at my confusion.

I retraced my thoughts. If there really were rules to the wishing worlds, then maybe—just maybe—if the orb went back to the place it came from, things would go back to the beginning, like hitting the reset button on a game console. Maybe the orb's return to the sea meant the wishing worlds were over, and we had been returned to the world as it was.

Splash! Splash!

A new sound came, joining those of the fireworks. Nazuna was cupping handfuls of seawater and throwing them against her face. She repeated the action over and over, like she was trying to wash some intangible thing away. Eventually, she stopped and turned toward me.

Her dripping face shone with the light of the fireworks. Her expression was mysterious. She seemed to be crying and laughing all at once. She spoke to me.

"...I guess this is where we say adieu."

"Huh?"

For a moment, the word didn't register. It was only because of the sorrow in her voice that I managed to parse the meaning.

My mind flashed with images of things that had happened in the "real world."

I saw the words FIREWORKS DISPLAY written on the calendar hanging in the bathroom. I heard the voice of the weather girl. I saw the yolk of the egg resting on top of my bowl of curry. I was racing down the slope on my worn-out bike with the ocean breeze whipping past. Nazuna stood at the water's edge with the glittering waves behind her. She was staring at my eyes in the classroom. She was lying along the edge of the pool in her swim-suit. The dragonfly rose from her breast and flew languidly into the sky. Nazuna's hand held out the orb for me to see. I heard her voice. *"You guys racing? I'm in."* The pool's water cascaded in great splashes as the three of us dived in. Nazuna swam ahead. I saw her from behind. She turned and headed back my way, and her eyes... She wore no goggles, and her eyes were looking at me.

Nazuna had been watching me. Always, since long ago, she'd been watching me...

I felt a dull pain in my right foot. I lifted it up out of the ocean water and saw there was a wound on the ankle. Skin had torn away, leaving an exposed patch that was light pink.

We came back... We really came back...to the world we started at...

I looked up. Nazuna was...staring at me, smiling. But in her eyes I could see drops welling up that weren't from the sea. It seemed they might come gushing out at any moment.

"Ahhhhhhhhhhhhhh!!!"

I hollered, throwing off my T-shirt and kicking off my shoes. Without any idea of what had come over me, I found myself run-ning into the water toward Nazuna.

Nazuna seemed taken aback by my abrupt cry. When I closed in, I tried to throw my arms around her in a great, big hug, but I stumbled when the sand dropped away beneath my feet more quickly than I'd expected. I ended up slamming into her and pushing us both underwater.

It would have been pitch-black under the surface had it not been for the shimmering fireworks blooming high above. The spray of sparks dancing through the sky blended in with the sight of the bubbles all around us. It felt like we were swimming among the fireworks themselves.

Everything moved in slow motion in this private world for Nazuna and me. Our bodies drifted about through the under-water fireworks. Nazuna reached forward and clasped both my hands. She slipped her fingers between mine and looked into my eyes.

I held mine open wide and stared back. I was seeing her face clearly under the water, without any goggles.

Her smiling face slowly drew near.

Her eyes closed, she pulled herself even closer, and then…she pressed her lips against mine.

"!!"

It was like I'd blown a fuse from her bold, unexpected action… the first *kiss* of my entire life! My first, instantaneous thought was about the sensation of her lips; they felt soft and squishy, like the yolk of a raw egg. But the thought had hardly registered before the panicked realization I'd just had—that I was *having* my first kiss, and suddenly I was dangerously low on air. I broke away from Nazuna's lips and pulled myself up to the surface, desperate for breath.

I stuck my head straight up toward the sky and opened my mouth to pull in a big lungful of fresh air. A joyous, round explosion filled the sky in greeting.

Turns out fireworks are *round from below…and round if you see them from the side, too…*

It was something I'd probably known all along. Perhaps at that moment, up on the top of Moshimo Lighthouse, Yusuke and the others were seeing that same firework from the side and having the same realization.

The thought prompted me to turn in the direction of the lighthouse. Just then, Nazuna surfaced within my field of view. Embarrassed, I looked away.

Even though she'd been the one to instigate the kiss, I didn't have any idea how I was supposed to look at her or act around her now that it had happened.

"Wow! It's gorgeous!!"

Nazuna paid my hesitation no mind. She nimbly pivoted in

the water so that she was now floating on her back, taking in the whole of the fireworks display.

Everything from her shoulders down sank gently into the water. Only her face remained above the surface.

"It's wonderful... It's like we're floating among the fireworks themselves..."

Nazuna's murmur echoed the thought I'd had under the water. My mind eased. I relaxed, floating on my back like her, and entrusted my body to the sea. The movement of the waves naturally carried the two of us near each other.

The night sky continued to fill with round firework explosions, but it seemed natural to me that they wouldn't last forever.

In another ten or twenty minutes, the show would be over. The people on the beach would head back to their houses. Yusuke and the others—probably at the lighthouse at that moment—would go home, too.

Even Nazuna and I would have to.

For two thirteen-year-olds like us, there was no other place to go back to.

Other worlds to escape to, like the ones we'd been to that day, didn't really exist.

"Hey, Norimichi."

Nazuna spoke to me, still looking up at the fireworks in the night sky.

"Hmm?"

I wanted to turn my head toward her, but I knew I'd get seawater in my nose and mouth. So I continued looking up like she did.

"I wonder what kind of world it will be, where we see each other next."

"..."

"I'll be looking forward to it."

With those words, Nazuna tilted herself onto her side and

began slowly swimming back to shore. Her receding figure blended in with the light of the fireworks reflected off the waves. It was such a beautiful sight—all I could do was watch.

Or perhaps I felt as if there was nothing I could say that would change that image of Nazuna swimming away.

Nazuna was headed toward the one and only true world, where there were no "do-overs," "what-ifs," or "if onlys," and she was going there at a calm and steady pace.

If… If only I was able to see Nazuna again… No matter what kind of world we were in when it happened, I'd let her know how I really felt.

Calling out just like I had each time the wishing orb was thrown, I shouted…

"Nazuna, I love you!!!!"

Postscript... Or Rather,
Some Parting Words.

Usually, I work as a director of television shows and movies...

That might be a jarring thing to hear at the beginning of a so-called postscript, where a reader might normally come to enjoy the last refrain of a novel just finished. But it is part of a story I would like to share.

Fireworks, Should We See it from the Side or the Bottom? was first created as a live-action television film twenty-four years ago.

When discussion began about remaking the live-action version as an animated film, I was chosen to write the screenplay. However, that screenplay ultimately came to include numerous differences from the original, including changes to the characters and setting, as well as the addition of entirely new segments to the latter part of the story.

Specifically, the ages of Norimichi and Nazuna were shifted from elementary school to junior high school; the one "wishing world" in the original was expanded to several in the animated film; and a brand-new element was introduced that hadn't existed at all in the live-action version: the "wishing orb"...

In short, the film was adjusted to fit the new medium... Many things about it are quite different from the worldview espoused by Mr. Iwai's original.

Later, when I was asked about writing the novelization, my initial response was a flat no. I'd never written a novel before. It seemed an impossible task for me.

However, a thought occurred that changed my mind:

As their creator, didn't I have a responsibility to the characters, settings, and later story developments that I'd allowed to diverge from the original film?

If so, I was determined to fulfill that responsibility. I agreed to tackle the unfamiliar format of novels.

Given that context, I'm afraid there must be a great many points where my expressions are crude or my words insufficient.

Surely many readers must have felt it peculiar when screenplay-like excerpts suddenly interrupted the text, far different from the typical format of a novel.

As the novel itself was written from the point of view of Norimichi, I was unsure how to handle scenes he neither was present for nor witnessed. My solution was to write them in the same way I had before: like a screenplay...

Excuses aside, my point is this:

This story originated as a live-action and then an animated film. It was created to be a cinematic experience. And that means the story itself is cinematic.

Though that might seem axiomatic, I expect some readers have read this book first, without having seen the live-action or animated films.

Of course, I'm thankful to those readers as well. But if at all possible, I'd like to encourage them to seek out the live-action and animated films to enjoy together with the novel.

I believe doing so will bring further depth to the scenery and characters those readers envisioned as they digested the novel, and that it will shine a light of understanding upon the points that an unskilled author like me failed to make clear.

In fact, I *urge* you to see the films!

I gave my all in writing this novel, but ultimately, the films better portray the subtle distance Norimichi feels toward girls and his inability to express those things, as a typical elementary or junior-high-aged boy would.

And last but not least, Nazuna!

Both the Nazuna of the live-action and the Nazuna of the animated film encapsulate a pinnacle of the endearment and charm of young love!

Therefore, I fervently hope you enjoy *Fireworks* as a set of three: the live-action film, the animated film, and the novelization!!!

Finally, I'd like to conclude with a few words to the father of this work, Mr. Shunji Iwai; to Director Akiyuki Shinbo and staff, who brought the animated film to the screen; to Mr. Genki Kawamura, who planned and produced the project; to all the individuals who were involved in the creation of both the live-action and animated films; and most of all, to all those who reached out to this book and took the time to read...

I love you!!!!!

May 2017
Hitoshi One

HAVE YOU BEEN TURNED ON TO LIGHT NOVELS YET?

IN STORES NOW!

SWORD ART ONLINE, VOL. 1–14
SWORD ART ONLINE, PROGRESSIVE 1–4

The chart-topping light novel series that spawned the explosively popular anime and manga adaptations!

MANGA ADAPTATION AVAILABLE NOW!

SWORD ART ONLINE © Reki Kawahara ILLUSTRATION: abec
KADOKAWA CORPORATION ASCII MEDIA WORKS

ACCEL WORLD, VOL. 1–14

Prepare to accelerate with an action-packed cyber-thriller from the bestselling author of *Sword Art Online*.

MANGA ADAPTATION AVAILABLE NOW!

ACCEL WORLD © Reki Kawahara ILLUSTRATION: HIMA
KADOKAWA CORPORATION ASCII MEDIA WORKS

SPICE AND WOLF, VOL. 1–19

A disgruntled goddess joins a traveling merchant in this light novel series that inspired the *New York Times* bestselling manga.

MANGA ADAPTATION AVAILABLE NOW!

SPICE AND WOLF © Isuna Hasekura ILLUSTRATION: Jyuu Ayakura
KADOKAWA CORPORATION ASCII MEDIA WORKS

WRONG TO TRY TO PICK UP GIRLS DUNGEON?, VOL. 1–11

would-be hero turns msel in distress in s hilarious send-up sword-and-sorcery pes.

NGA ADAPTATION AILABLE NOW!

Wrong to Try to Pick Up Girls Dungeon? © Fujino Omori / reative Corp.

FUJINO OMORI

ILLUSTRATION BY SUZUHITO YASUDA

ANOTHER

The spine-chilling horror novel that took Japan by storm is now available in print for the first time in English—in a gorgeous hardcover edition.

MANGA ADAPTATION AVAILABLE NOW!

Another © Yukito Ayatsuji 2009/ KADOKAWA CORPORATION, Tokyo

RTAIN MAGICAL INDEX, VOL. 1–16

ce and magic collide as Japan's popular light novel franchise s its English-language debut.

A ADAPTATION AVAILABLE NOW!

TAIN MAGICAL INDEX © Kazuma Kamachi TRATION: Kiyotaka Haimura KAWA CORPORATION ASCII MEDIA WORKS

Another

yukito ayatsuji

1

KAZUMA KAMACHI

ILLUSTRATION BY KIYOTAKA HAIMURA

A Certain Magical Index

VISIT YENPRESS.COM TO CHECK OUT ALL THE TITLES IN OUR NEW LIGHT NOVEL INITIATIVE AND...

GET YOUR YEN ON!

www.YenPress.com